But From Thine Eyes: Scintillating historical drama set in an Edwardian English theatre

(His Majesty's Theatre Book 2)

Christina Britton Conroy

First published by Endeavour Press Ltd in 2017.
This edition published by Lume Books in 2020.

Table of Contents

Chapter 1

London, Friday, December 18, 1903

The train pulled into St. Pancras Station at noon. Steam poured from the tracks as the huge locomotive jarred to a halt, rocking the passenger cars behind it. Dozens of compartment doors flew open and hundreds of passengers stepped onto the platform. Elisa Roundtree clutched her small traveling bag and wove her way along the crowded platform. Outside the station, hansom cabs stood ready for hire. They looked warm and safe, and expensive. She needed to save her money.

She hurried to a porter loading luggage onto a wheeled cart, and begged, "Excuse me, sir. Do you know how I might find His Majesty's Theatre? It's in a place called Haymarket."

" 'aymarket omnibus stops just there, Miss." He pointed to the street corner.

"Thanks very much." Elisa queued behind other shivering travellers waiting for the omnibus. She pulled up her coat collar and pinched it around her throat. Then she swung the hem aside and checked her pale green skirt. The folds of heavy muslin were wrinkled, but clean.

Two huge horses pulled an omnibus near the curb. Afraid of missing her stop, she paid her fare, then sat near the conductor. She had never seen a large city with so many fine motorcars and carriages. She gasped at the height and closeness of the buildings, and the rich clothing on pedestrians crowding the sidewalks.

After a few stops, the conductor called, "Haymarket!" then, "Charles Street!" He leaned into her. "Look Miss, There's His Majesty's Theatre. Herbert Beerbohm Tree opened the place, about five years back. Tree's touring America now. Leased it to Jeremy O'Connell."

"Oh, I see. Thanks very much." She stepped off the omnibus into a slop of mud and horse dung. Gingerly tiptoeing through the muck, she balanced her traveling bag with one hand and lifted her skirt with the other.

Directly in front of her stood a huge ornate building made from light gray stone. Two-story high Corinthian pillars, arched windows, and delicate stone carvings decorated the front wall. Several stories higher, a large green dome gleamed. The words, HIS MAJESTY'S THEATRE, were chiselled above the wide entrance. Several wide double doors were closed. One stood open. A placard read:

TONIGHT at 8:00
Mr. JEREMY O'CONNELL
Miss KATHERINE STEWART
in MACBETH

Only a few feet away, the great actor-manager Jeremy O'Connell staged his own productions, played leading roles, and trained brilliant young actors. Elisa swallowed hard. "I'm a schoolgirl, not an actress. What am I doing here?"

"Ticket queue ends back there, Miss." A man pointed to a line of people curved around the building.

Elisa stammered, "Oh n'no, thank you. I'm looking for the stage entrance."

The man snickered, "Which one are you in love wiv? O'Connell or Freeman? 'round the corner y' go." He pointed to his right and walked away chuckling.

Elisa's cheeks burned as she followed his directions. Half-way around the block even more people were gathered. A small sign was painted on a plain wooden door:

HIS MAJESTY'S THEATRE
STAGE ENTRANCE

Her legs felt weak as she pushed through the crowd, and slowly opened the door. Just inside, an old man sat behind a high wooden desk. Unsmiling, he looked up from his newspaper. "Yes, Miss?"

"Please, sir, I'm looking for Michael Burns." Her voice sounded very small.

The old man smiled. "Right-i-o. Michael said a young lady was coming, and to send her 'round to the pub. Just go back out and make a left. You can't miss it."

"Thank you. You're very kind."

He nodded as she opened the stage door and hurried out. Her pale green skirt caught on the edge and she scolded herself. *Slow down!* She closed her eyes and took a deep breath. She only had one frock. She mustn't tear it. Once outside, she looked left and saw a comical sign hanging over the pub entrance. *THE ACTRESS AND VILLAIN* was painted in large letters. Under the name was a painting of footlights and stage curtains framing an evil looking man stabbing a fat woman with long hair.

Below the sign were double doors with brass handles. She pulled one side open, and walked through heavy curtains into a medium sized dining area. To her left was a long service bar. Tables stood in the middle and booths with benches lined the sides. Small windows allowed slight sunlight and ventilation. Popping coal fires burned in fireplaces at both ends of the room, and a haze of tobacco smoke hung in the warm, motionless air. A pleasant aroma of hot food made her empty stomach rumble. Working people of all ages were eating, drinking, and smoking.

" 'ello, 'ello, what's this then?"

Elisa was startled by a pair of flashing dark eyes. A funny looking little man, with a thick bowl cut of grey hair, smiled up at her. "If you please, sir, I'm looking for Michael Burns."

He pretended shock and jumped back. "'Sir,' is it? Ooh, I do like that." He was adorable and she laughed. He looked toward the back of the pub. "Michael!" He called in a light, resonate voice that easily carried into the adjoining saloon area. "Lovely lady to see you." He turned back to Elisa, made a comical bow, and walked outside.

A young man stepped up. "Miss Roundtree?"

"Yes."

He extended his hand. "Splendid to meet you. I'm Michael Burns." He was tall and thin, with copper hair and green eyes, like hers.

Elisa happily shook his hand. "How-do-you-do?"

"Sorry I couldn't meet your train."

"That's quite all right. It was easy finding the theatre."

He looked her up-and-down. "You're as beautiful as Rob said. Are you hungry?"

She blushed at the compliment. "Famished -- and, please call me Elisa."

He chose a table off to the side and took her coat. "Chicken pie is the Friday regular. It's not bad, if you like chicken."

"Thank you. That would be lovely."

"Won't be a minute." He loped to the bar, and quickly returned, carrying a tray. "I brought lemonade. I hope that's all right. Didn't think you'd want anything stronger before an audition." He put down two glasses, and plates of steaming pie and peas. A man at another table sent Michael a thumbs-up. Elisa looked startled and Michael laughed. "Don't mind this lot. They're all theatre folk. You'll get to know them soon enough."

She thirstily drank the lemonade. "Thanks. That's lovely."

They ate their lunch, and Michael chatted about their mutual friend, Robert Dennison. His schoolboy stories were funny and she liked him. She was barely done eating when the wall clock struck the half-hour.

Michael sprang up. "It's one-thirty. We'd better go."

He helped her with her coat and she followed nervously, back into the theatre and onto the huge empty stage. She felt a rush of adrenaline as she moved far down onto the apron. Only two of the twenty footlights burned, as she looked into the dark stalls. Michael led her into an off-stage dressing room, and she wrinkled her nose. The stench of greasepaint and lacquer made her eyes water. The walls were whitewashed and the floor was clean. Assorted stage makeup and a pile of clean rags lay on the dressing table.

She looked at her filthy shoes. "May I use one of those?"

"Use whatever you need."

It took some effort to scrape off the dried muck. Seeing her reflection, she tossed her coat over a chair. "I look a fright." She removed three combs, and her mass of copper hair cascaded down past her waist.

Michael gasped. "Don't tie that up, for goodness sake, leave it long."

She was surprised, but took his advice and brushed out the tangles. Taking a tortoiseshell comb, she pulled one side away from her face. Michael chose a medium brown charcoal stick. "Stand still." Gently holding her chin, he darkened her nearly translucent eyebrows and lashes. "When Eric Bates sees you, he'll think he died and went to heaven." He lightly rouged her cheeks and lips.

"Who is Eric Bates?"

"The business manager… and an actor… actually, his wife keeps the books… never mind about that now. I'll leave you to do your prep'."

She grabbed Michael's arm, "Please don't go. I don't know what to do. Please help me." Weeks of buried tension exploded. Tears spilled down her cheeks and onto her dress.

Michael was startled, but used to hysterical actors. He took her by the shoulders. "Just stop it! Stop it this instant! Recite your monologue. Now!"

Juliet's words poured out in one meaningless string: "Gallopapeceyoufiery-footedsteedstowardsPhoebus'lodging…"

"Stop! Start again. Slowly."

Gasping, she did as she was told. "*Gallop apace, you fiery-footed steeds,*

Towards Phoebus' lodging…"

She finished, breathing hard, feeling calmer. "Thank you, Michael. I'm sorry."

"Shall I do your eyes again?"

"Yes. Please."

As Michael wiped away the teary smudges and darkened her eyelashes, two-dozen young women crowded the backstage area.

A thin young man with an equally thin voice held a list of names. "All the young ladies please take a seat. I'm Eddy Edwards the stage-manager. Please answer when you hear your name." He held up a list and squinted to read. "Miss Jamison?"

"Yes, sir." A plump girl appeared.

Eddy scratched his over-large nose. "Miss Andrews?"

"Here, sir," and on and on until finally, "Miss Roundtree?"

"Yes, sir."

Eddy continued, "Misters Bates and O'Connell will be hearing the auditions. There will probably be other busybodies peering around, but don't mind them."

Michael whispered to Elisa, "Jeremy O'Connell's staging the play and playing Prospero. He wants a fairy spirit, or something like that, to shadow him, on stage, throughout the entire play. You're by far the prettiest girl here. You're sure to be engaged."

*

The night before, a new production of *Macbeth* had opened to brilliant reviews. Weeks of planning and rehearsals had turned actor-manager Jeremy O'Connell into a heartless dictator. Nothing less than perfection had been acceptable from the actors on-stage and the army of workers slaving backstage. After the opening night curtain fell, Jeremy, business-manager-actor Eric Bates, most of the cast and crew had huddled in theatre stalls, waiting for their reviews. When the papers gloriously sailed in, each notice better than the last, Jeremy and Eric had celebrated long and hard.

At 2:30 the next afternoon, the two men sat in the center of the dark theatre, hung-over and exhausted. Eric lay across three red velvet seats, not noticing dried mud from his boots dusting the expensive fabric. Forty-two and overweight, his graying hair was thin and greasy.

He rubbed his burning eyes and yawned. "Was it my brainless idea to hold auditions the day after an opening?"

Actor-manager Jeremy O'Connell nodded, then dozed in his seat. He had recently celebrated his fortieth birthday and, on most days, was fantastically handsome. He was very tall, very thin, and very fit. His dark hair was cut short and combed back off his clean shaven face. Since actors wore false beards and moustaches, they were the only men in London with no facial hair. Last night Jeremy's dark eyes had been brilliantly piercing. Today they were red and sore. He longed for a hot toddy and a soft bed.

Their task seemed terribly simple: Find a pretty girl to stand on stage. After a dozen common girls recited dull poems and monologues, Eric shuddered. "Good Lord, Jerry, aren't there any pretty girls in London?"

Jeremy fluttered a hand. "Well dear heart, you would know that better than I, I am sure."

"Bloody pouf!" Eric laughed and shook his head. When Jeremy shrugged majestically, Eric laughed louder and called to the stage, "Eddy, is that the lot?"

"One more, sir."

Jeremy pulled the list of names from the floor, squinted to read the last one, and dropped his head into his hand. "Eric. Her name is Roundtree. I hope she does not look like a round tree." They dissolved into hysterical laughter.

A girl walked gracefully on stage. She smiled radiantly. The men sat up and stared. She was taller than the others, very slim, very pale, with a flowing mane of light-red hair hanging along one side of her face and down past her waist. The other side of her hair was clipped back, revealing a beautifully sculptured cheekbone and huge, glowing eyes. She wore a pale green frock suited for a schoolgirl, and looked very young despite her height.

Apprentice actor Rory Cook shuffled up the aisle bringing mugs of steaming tea. He handed one to Jeremy, saw the girl, and nearly spilled the scalding liquid. Amused by his reaction, Jeremy passed the mug to Eric and took the other. Rory slid into a seat behind the older men. The girl took a deep breath, and recited Juliet's soliloquy.

"Gallop apace, you fiery-footed steeds,
Towards Phoeobus' lodging…"

When her inflection moved up and down with the sing-song pattern of the verse, Jeremy sadly shook his head. Most young people were taught to memorize the words, with no thought to their meaning. Eric leaned toward him. "What do you think?"

Jeremy raised an eyebrow. "She looks like a nymph. She'll do."

"She can't act."

"She doesn't have to."

The monologue droned on, but Jeremy could not take his eyes off the stunningly beautiful girl. Her inflections were dreadful; her vocal technique nonexistent, and her school perfect diction was flavored with a Yorkshire accent. Her voice had a natural resonance that carried surprisingly well. Her face and figure were absolute perfection.

"Right." Eric yawned. "She's a friend of Michael Burns. Wants to be an apprentice."

"Really? Where is she going to live?"

"They live at Potter's."

Jeremy spat out, "Mrs. Potter's boardinghouse is filth, and the meals are absolute slop. This girl speaks like a lady. Her posture is perfect, she obviously has breeding, and she cannot live there."

Eric shook his head. "Come on Jerry, you know Hilda's rule. If an apprentice has money, she can do better. If not, it's Potter's."

Jeremy pictured Eric's hard-faced wife Hilda Bates. The lady was an excellent business manager, but penny-pinched to the extreme. He turned to see twenty-year-old Rory Cook stare adoringly at the stage. Male patrons would have the same reaction. He wanted this girl and silently prayed she could afford decent lodgings. Rory lived at Mrs. Potter's boardinghouse. A year ago, he gave up his inheritance, an Oxford education, and future career as a solicitor to become an apprentice actor working for no wages. He shared a bed with two other apprentice actors. Rory had arrived wearing a beautifully tailored suit. His golden hair had been smartly trimmed and his collar sparkling white. Today, he wore that same suit, but the fine wool was torn and stained. His hair was greasy and his collar was gone.

When the girl finished, Eric called out, "Thank you, Miss Round..." He tried to say, round tree, and started to laugh. "Mr. Edwards, come here a minute." The girl curtsied and Eddy nearly knocked her over as he bounded off the apron into the stalls. Eric whispered, "Jerry, you won't mind having her in your class?"

"No, not at all. I should be able to teach her something. If not she'll get discouraged and leave at the end of the run. Either way the lads will enjoy playing scenes with her. They've had their fill of Meg and Peg."

"Our resident alley cats." Eric chuckled, thinking of their two female apprentices. Since they received no wages, they worked... elsewhere.

Eddy leapt up. "Yes sirs."

"Ah Mr. Edwards, ask Miss, what is it, Round-tree...to come to my office. Thank the rest and send them home."

Jeremy shook his head. "We must change that girl's name. Let's get a drink."

Rory hurdled from his seat. "Mr. O'Connell, Mr. Bates, she's beautiful. She speaks like a lady and she's going to be working here." He raised his eyes to heaven. "There really is a God. Thank you -- Thank you."

Jeremy playfully pushed him back down.

Chapter 2

Elisa and Michael waited on a wooden bench in front of Eric Bates's office. Michael spoke carefully. "From this second on, you cannot be too careful when you deal with Jeremy O'Connell. His opinion will be the most important thing in your life. If he likes you, he'll make your life hell. If he doesn't like you, it'll be double hell."

Elisa caught her breath and Michael continued wearily, "I respect the man, but I don't like him. He's a brilliant actor and teacher, but he can be cruel. Especially if he believes an actor has talent." He laughed sadly. "We have a saying, 'When it comes to Jerry, never contradict and never agree.'" He yawned. "I'm sorry. We had an opening, last night. I celebrated too much and slept too little." He looked down the stairs. "Where are those bug'..?" He bit his tongue and checked his watch.

Elisa pleaded, "You've been so kind. Please go and rest. I'll be all right."

He shook his head. "If you're engaged, which I think you will be, you'll be living at Mrs. Potter's boardinghouse. There's a lot more I need to tell you."

*

Eric Bates and Jeremy O'Connell had their drink at *The Actress and Villain*, and returned to the theatre. Just inside the stage entrance, they heard angry voices. Stage-manager Eddy Edwards rushed towards them.

"Sirs, we've a bit of a problem with Mick Tanner."

Eric shook his head. "Mick Tanner, my butcher's assistant? Whatever does he want?"

"He wants to be in *The Tempest*. He heard you were engaging supers and…"

Jeremy's mouth dropped open. Mick Tanner was a wonderful-looking dimwit he had thrown out of his acting class. Tall as Jeremy, with a broader chest and powerful shoulders, dark eyes blazing under heavy brows, Mick stood at the foot of the stairs, glaring daggers. "That's righ', Mr. Bates. You promised I'd get a par' in your next play, so…"

Suddenly sober, Jeremy smiled engagingly. "Eric, what a pity, you forgot to mention the availability of Mr. Tanner. All the roles in *The Tempest* have been cast. This is a terrible shame. There simply is nothing available. I am so very sorry, Mr. Tanner. Perhaps next season – or better still, why don't you inquire at the Lyceum? Their productions are far grander than ours. They employ a great many more people, and..."

"Oi' tried the Lyceum. They're full up. I don' need lines this time. I'll be a super for y', for no pay. Please, Mr. O'Connell, gi' me another chance. I know I can..."

Jeremy shrugged benignly. "I am so sorry, Mr. Tanner."

"You're no' sorry! You think I'm just a butcher's boy, a stupid piece of shit, good fer nothing' but crushin' bones all day, not good enough for yer fancy..." He lunged toward Jeremy, and two strong backstage workers dragged him from the building. Mick howled, "Oi'll be back in this theatre. Just see if Oi'm not. Oi'll be back and you'll both be sorry."

Hearts pounding, Jeremy and Eric started up the stairs. The girl and actor Michael Burns waited in the dim hall. They both sprang to attention. The girl was slightly shorter than Michael, but their coloring and builds were identical. Both had light-red hair, green eyes, and very pale skin. The girl's small breasts and slim hips meant she could easily pass for a boy, and Jeremy's mind raced with ideas for staging *The Tempest*. Michael stepped aside as the girl followed the older men into Eric's office.

Once behind his desk, Eric rubbed his bloodshot eyes and concentrated. The girl perched nervously on the edge of a chair. Jeremy leaned out an open window, gulping cold fresh air in an effort to stay awake. Eric cleared his throat. "Miss..." he shook his head. "What are we going to call you? Your real name will not do." She stared blankly and he asked. "What is your Christian name?"

"Elisa."

He strained to hear. "What? Eliza?"

"No sir, it's pronounced El-ee-za. It's German."

"Too difficult. What shall it be, Mr. O'Connell?"

Jeremy was half asleep. "What, sorry? Oh, I don't know. Elizabeth... Eliza... Elly."

Eric looked up. "Elly. That's good... umm, all right, Elly... Elly Round... Room... Reynolds... Reems... Let me see... Elly Tree...

Trees... Treemont... He looked at the ceiling. "Not 'Ellen Terry.' We've already got one of those." He laughed at his reference to the great actress. "Elly Green... Field... Fields... Fielding. How's that? Elly Fielding."

The girl repeated the name. "Elly Fielding – Elly Fielding." A lovely smile spread across her pale lips.

"Do you live in London Miss... Fielding?"

"No sir." She looked surprised.

"Have you acquired lodgings?"

"No sir."

"Do you have a private income?"

"No sir." Now she looked frightened.

"Have you any people in London who can offer you shelter?"

"No sir. I have no one at all." Her narrow shoulders sagged as if this were a final defeat.

"Not to worry." Taking his pen, Eric scratched a few lines onto a slip of paper and handed it to her. "Take this over to Mrs. Potter. She will take care of you."

"Thank you, sir." She read the address.

Mrs. Potter
5 Charles II Street

Jeremy muttered angrily, "Mrs. Potter's..."

Eric continued, "Check with Eddy Edwards the stage-manager. You met him earlier. He will give you a schedule." He leaned over the desk and spoke seriously. "Miss Fielding, apprentices are here to learn. Training plus room-and-board are your wages. You will receive no salary. You will attend all possible rehearsals whether or not you are in the scene, work in both the costume and the wig-shop, and attend as many performances as possible. Once a week you will take an acting class taught by my esteemed colleague..." Dozing against the window frame, Jeremy jerked to attention hearing, "...Mr. O'Connell, and you will rehearse with your scene partners any time it does not interfere with your other duties. You will receive only breakfast and tea at the boardinghouse, so you need to find another source of income if you wish to eat lunch or supper, is that clear?"

15

The girl they now called Elly Fielding sat rigid with attention. She stammered, "Y'Yes sir, I think so, sir."

"Good. You can start by watching tonight's performance of The Scottish Play. After Mr. O'Connell has had a nap and his tea, I think you may be amazed by his recovery – Jerry, go have a lie-down."

"Right-i-o." Half-blind with fatigue, Jeremy staggered from the room.

Eric saw Michael through the open door. "Mr. Burns, before you go for *your* nap, will you be so kind as to take Miss Fielding over to Potter's?"

"Who sir?"

"This is our new apprentice, Miss Elly Fielding."

*

Michael slowly led Elisa back down stairs to the stage entrance. Practically asleep, it took all his energy to put one foot in front of the other. The old man was still behind his desk.

"Adams, this is our new apprentice, Elly Fielding."

Adams smiled and extended his hand. Elisa, now Elly, took it happily.

"So you made it Miss. My 'artiest congratulations. Welcome aboard, I 'ope you'll be 'appy 'ere."

Elly was so pleased by the old man's words, she wanted to kiss him. "Thank you so much. You're very kind."

Michael checked the call board. "Eddy Edwards's gone. He'll give you a schedule later." He walked on, then leaned against the large stage door and almost fell as it gave way. Elly quickly followed. Once outside, he pushed through a crowd of autograph seekers.

Elly was thrilled. "Are there always crowds like this?"

"Sometimes. The fans want to see Jeremy O'Connell and Katherine Stewart. Shop girls love Owen Freeman. They don't care about the rest of us."

He led her along Haymarket, past the front of the theatre, a bookseller, and photographer's shop, before making a quick right turn onto Charles II Street. The houses were small, but clean and well kept. Halfway up the block, he stopped in front of a dilapidated red-brick building. It looked out of place on the pleasant street. The front door glass was shattered into a spider web pattern, and almost every window was cracked or boarded over. Broken wooden stairs led up to a battered wooden door.

BOARDING HOUSE

S. Potter, Proprietor
INQUIRE WITHIN

Elly froze, staring at the house. Michael saw her reaction. "Let's walk
on a little." They continued a few houses down, and sat on a low stone
wall. Elly had no idea what he was going to say, but felt sure it would not
be good.

Finally he spoke. "Have you got any money?"

She was startled. "A little."

"Hide it. If anyone asks, tell them you haven't got any. Do you have
any cases?"

"Just this." She held up her small traveling bag. "The rest of my
clothes are being shipped with Robert's paintings."

"You two are something." He pictured art-master Robert Dennison
beside this lovely schoolgirl and wondered what they were to each other.
"You only have the one frock?"

"For now. Is that all right? I might be able to fetch the boxes from the
art gallery."

"Actually, that's very good." He took in a deep breath and let it out
very slowly.   "Listen to me and remember what I am going to tell
you." Elly's eyes grew large as
he told his story.

"Rob probably told you that we ran away from school, together. We
were eighteen. He went to Paris to paint. I joined a run-down theatre
company and toured the provinces for four years. I was so desperate to
join a first-class theatre, Eric Bates offered me an unpaid apprenticeship,
and I took it.

"After one month living there," he pointed to Potter's, "I was ready to
go back on the road. Fortunately, Jeremy O'Connell saw my worth, and
convinced Hilda Bates to pay me a starvation wage. It's taken another
three years for her to pay me a real wage. You were the prettiest girl they
saw today, but if you left, they would easily find another. You're not an
actress, so you have no power."

He rubbed his eyes and continued very softly. "Potter's is a dangerous
place. Nothing you own is safe: your clothes, your shoes, your hair
brush, and especially your money. Sleep with your purse around your

neck and never, ever, let anyone see it. For a while you'll be wearing the same frock every day. That's good. They'll think you're poor."

"But, I am poor."

"Not as poor as some. You need to make up a story and stick to it. Tell them you're an orphan and spent all your money on this one frock and the train fare, or some such thing. When your boxes arrive, you'll have to hide your other clothes. God knows where." He crossed his arms and leaned his head on his hand. "I can already see Meg and Peg coming to rehearsals wearing lovely frocks several inches too long."

"Meg and Peg?"

"Your fellow apprentices. Tarts, the both of them. You'll probably share a room."

Elly's mouth fell open, as Michael continued, "The food is inedible. Anytime someone offers you a meal, accept without question. If a bloke buys you a meal and wants too high a repayment, eat, run away, and avoid him in the future. You need to survive. You need to keep your looks and you can only do that if you eat and sleep. Be clever and stay alert. Are you coming to the show tonight?"

He had startled her again. "Why, yes. Of course."

"Good, come backstage and I'll introduce you around."

She watched, as he seemed to sleepwalk back to Haymarket and catch his omnibus. Making herself smile, Elly walked to the boardinghouse door, knocked, and waited. After three tries, a pleasant looking, shabbily dressed old woman opened the door.

"Yes, what can I do for y'?"

"Please ma'am, I'm a new apprentice at His Majesty's Theatre. Are you Mrs. Potter?"

The old woman raised one eyebrow as she looked Elly up-and-down. "Aye, I'm Potter." Elly gave her the note from Eric Bates. She read it silently. " 'ave you got any money?"

"No, I'm sorry."

"You'd better come along then." Mrs. Potter turned abruptly and went inside.

Elly followed her into a dingy entrance hall, and stumbled as her heel caught in a carpet tear. To keep from falling, she braced herself on a bad smelling old coat hanging on the wall. A dozen coat hooks stood empty. How many people lived in this house? A wooden crate sat on the floor, piled with candle stubs. Obviously, the house had no gas lights. The drawing room walls were unevenly covered with yellowed wallpaper. The ceiling was cracked and split. A large hole in the plaster exposed a rotting beam. The few pieces of ancient furniture were torn and dirty, and worm-eaten floorboards showed through a threadbare carpet.

Mrs. Potter stopped at the foot of the stairs. Clutching the once dark-stained banister, now worn smooth and blond, she carefully placed her right foot on the first step, pulled herself up on her right leg, and dragged the left leg up after it. This procedure was repeated on each step, so it took some time to reach the second floor. The stairs creaked loudly and the air was damp with mold.

Finally on the upstairs landing, Mrs. Potter said, "You'll be up there with the other girls," and started a slow ascent to the next floor.

Following her, Elly had plenty of time to read name plates on the doors. One had three metal slots nailed to it, with a soiled piece of paper in each. Printed in childlike, block letters were: MR. RED; MR. SINKLAR; MR. COOK. Further down were two doors with MRS. LIN and MR. STRLING. Finally reaching the next floor, Elly saw two doors with name slots. Mrs. Potter removed one slip of paper.

"This one's out with the pantomime, no telling if she'll be back." Turning the slip over, she slid the blank side into the name slot, pulled a pencil stub from her pocket, and marked the paper.

When she stood back, Elly read the names, MISS OMALY; MISS LAMOOR; MISS FELDING. Elly assumed that "Felding" was supposed to be Fielding, but said nothing. Mrs. Potter opened the unlocked door.

"You'll be in 'ere with Meg and Peg, them's good girls, once you know 'em."

Elly looked into the room. She wanted to scream. Great chunks of plaster were missing from the walls and ceiling. Layers of moldy water stains smeared over the gaps. Dirt crusted into the floor and wind whistled sharply through the shattered window-glass. Even from the doorway she felt a draft. Soiled clothing, including undergarments, were scattered on the bed, over two broken chairs, a small three-legged table, and a sparsely filled wardrobe missing both doors. A chamber pot sat in the middle of the floor. It was empty, but certainly not clean, and the bed linen was filthy.

Elly took a deep breath, forced a smile and fought back tears. "Are we, all three, to sleep in the one bed, Mrs. Potter?"

"Right-i-o, m' girl. All the better to keep you warm." With that, the old woman turned and started her painful decent down the two flights of rickety stairs.

Elly stood in the hall, staring into her room, willing it to improve. She walked tentatively through the doorway, and shivered. It was just as cold inside as it was out. There was a sooty potbellied stove in the middle of the room, but no fuel to burn in it. Mrs. Potter's words rang in her ears, "All the better to keep you warm." But the bed! The sheet was gray and the pillows appeared to be encrusted with something. Using two fingers, she carefully pulled back the thin blanket. The sheet was one continuous pattern of yellow, brown, and gray stains. A rancid smell wafted up. She quickly dropped the blanket, and held her nose.

Clutching her bag, she ran from the room and up the final set of stairs. The ceiling was low and slanting. There was a single door, opening into a dark attic, thick with dust. Tiny beams of daylight shone through uneven slanting rafters. Her eyes quickly adjusted, and she made out some broken furniture and an old chest. She gave the lid a mighty heave. The hinges complained loudly and an intoxicating aroma of cedar wood filled the room. Inside was a ragged, sweet smelling quilt. Elly wrapped it around herself, lay on the floor, and was very quickly asleep.

BANG! BANG! BANG! Elly woke with a fright. How long had she been asleep? It took her only a moment to remember where she was and run onto the landing. The banging was uneven but continuous. She looked over the railing and saw the top of Mrs. Potter's head, three flights below.

Mrs. Potter yelled, "Mrs. Lynn, Y' tea is ready." She banged on a sauce pan with a wooden spoon, listened, then shrieked again, "Mrs. Lynn, Y' tea is ready."

One flight up, a door opened. A wiry old lady with flaming-red hair danced into the hall. She looked over the banister and yelled back, "IS IT TEA THEN?"

"Yes, come down y' deaf old bat."

"Oh lovely. Here I come." Mrs. Lynn trotted downstairs.

Elly was very hungry and felt good after her rest. She hurried downstairs and followed voices through the drawing room, into the dining room. Around a long table sat the flaming Mrs. Lynn, two scruffy young men, an old man, two other poorly-dressed women, one middle-aged, the other very old, and two rough-looking young women, she guessed were Meg and Peg.

Mrs. Potter cut thin slices from a loaf of hard bread. No one at the table seemed to notice Elly as they grabbed for the bowl of cold drippings, and dug out meager servings for their bread. Each had their own small saucer of watery jelly for pudding.

Elly sat down to a cracked plate with a thin slice of hard bread, and took the nearly empty drippings bowl. She was fond of roasted meat drippings, but this looked and smelled foul. Whatever the food was, it was survival of the fittest. She would not be late again. Mrs. Potter poured tea into chipped mugs. It was very hot and heavily laced with milk and sugar. Too sweet for Elly's taste, but her starving body craved it. She drank it down and asked for more. Listening to conversations, she quickly distinguished Meg from Peg.

Meg was tall, blond, plump, and loud. She had a very large bosom and a very low cut frock. Elly forced her fascinated eyes away. She had never seen anyone show that much naked flesh and it was only tea time. Meg spoke in a loud, raspy voice, and made eyes at all the men. She could have been pretty, but her yellow hair was bleached dry and brittle. Her fair skin was stained with dark rouge and lip color. Heavy charcoal darkened her naturally light eyes and made her look hard. She laughed loudly at the men's bad jokes.

Peg was short, scrawny, and dark. She wore no rouge. Black lines around her eyes made them appear huge. Her thick dark hair was tied back with a ribbon, emphasizing her pale, sunken cheeks. Totally silent, she ate as much as she could get.

The two older ladies were mother and daughter. The elder one drifted in a constant demented haze, focused on nothing, and said nothing. The daughter force-fed the old lady mouthfuls of bread and lard.

An old man sitting on Elly's right gave her a slight nod and a smile. The old woman with flaming red hair smiled, sipped her tea, and said nothing.

Two young men across the table behaved like bad school boys, teasing the girls. Words Elly had never heard above a whisper were hurled back and forth across the table like tennis balls. One young man, tall and wiry, with a deep rumbling voice, reached a remarkably long arm over to Peg's plate and tried to lift her jelly. Her spoon came down on his hand with a quick vengeance.

"Y' bleedin', ugly ape, keep yer 'ands to yer self."

This set off howls of laughter.

A short, chubby young man, with a round face and a mass of curly black hair, called, "Go up one, Peg. Teacher gives full marks for that."

Peg scowled at him. "Y' bloody, stupid sod. Don't y' know yet that m' name's Marguerite Lamoor? Not flamin' Peg?"

A voice sounded from the drawing room, as a good-looking, rather short, young blond man hung up his coat. "'Flaming' Peg!' Oh, that's good, isn't it? Suits her, don't y' think chaps?"

He strode into the dining room and an empty tea mug flew at his head. He caught it easily and tossed it to another man. Peg lunged at him with outstretched claws. He seized her arms, flipping her aside like a rag doll.

Peg hissed like a cat, and backed from the room spitting insults. "You buggerin' piece of shit, I'll kill y' some day!" She seized her coat, threw open the front door, ran out, slamming the door after her.

Meg sat primly. "She will kill y' some day, Rory Cook. And I wouldn't blame 'er, after what y' done to 'er."

Rory glared at her. "And what did I do then, eh? Nothing you've never done yourself, eh? Just because she was daft enough to get in trouble. That was none of my doing. It wasn't mine. She's had half of London. Could have been anybody's."

The elderly daughter roughly lifted her aged mother from her chair and pulled her toward the front door. "Come along mother, it's time for our walk."

Elly cowered in her chair. Who were these people? Was she really going to live with them? Michael's words flooded back. "Potter's is a dangerous place."

Rory stomped back to the dining room. Now that the table was half-empty, he saw lovely Elly sitting on the far side. Her eyes were wide, her shoulders hunched, and her hands clutched under the table. Rory's mouth dropped open.

She hesitantly looked up, meeting his apologetic eyes.

He nervously licked his lips. "That wasn't much of a welcome, Miss. I hope you can forgive me." His voice was beautiful and his diction impeccable.

She stared nervously.

The chubby fellow's good-natured laugh broke the tension. "Don't worry, Miss. Rory's a good chap. When he arrived, he was a gentleman. He's just been too long among us scum. I'm Lester Reid, a vicar's son, believe it or not: fourteen months a prisoner at Potter's."

Everyone laughed except Elly.

Lester's smile was sweet. "Look at the poor girl, she's terrified. It's really not so bad. You'll be fine, once you've settled in." He reached out his hand.

Elly gratefully shook it. "Thanks. You're very nice. I'm Elis'…Elly, Elly Fielding."

Meg sighed. " 'at's Peg's problem. She never did se'le in. We cum 'ere about the same time, wha' was it, two-year-ago now? She was gettin' good parts and all. There was talk o' puttin' 'er on salary. Then she went and got 'erself in trouble."

"It wasn't mine," Rory spoke through clenched teeth.

" 'oosever it was, she wanted it. Mr. Bates made 'er get rid o' it. Paid fer it, Oi think."

Meg turned to Elly. "My name is Margaret O'Mally. Them's what knows me calls me Meg."

With inappropriate formality, Meg extended a limp hand, palm down. "Very pleased to meet you, Oi'm sure."

Elly choked back a laugh as she clasped Meg's fish-like appendage. "Delighted, Miss O'Mally."

Rory walked around the table, offered his hand, and looked into her eyes. "I'm Rory Cook. Again, please, try to forgive my most unforgivable behaviour."

Feeling very uncomfortable, Elly accepted his hand. "How-do-you-do?" She looked into his soft blue eyes and felt herself blush.

The old gentleman spoke next. "My name is Peter Sterling. I'm the veteran here. Eight years, twelve maybe? Can't quite remember."

The young people laughed at his joke.

"Used to be an actor, m' dear. Can't remember m' lines anymore. Good for nothing, that's what old Pete is."

Rory shook his head. "I've seen the photos, Peter. You were a great actor."

"Too long ago, boy." Peter laughed. "Now, the great actor carries spears and bows a lot. I earn a-pound-a-week and all the slop Mrs. Potter can feed me." He raised his hands as if acknowledging applause. "And this darling deaf damsel," he indicated the sweet, old red-headed woman, "has become the lady of my old age."

Elly smiled at deaf Mrs. Lynn and studied her hair. How did she get it so red? She turned to the tall gangly actor.

"Oh gosh, sorry, I'm Todd Sinclair." His voice was wonderfully low, but he giggled like a schoolgirl. "How-d'-you-do." He extended an overlong paw. Elly shook his soft, moist hand. He seemed nice, but odd.

The clock struck seven and all the actors stood at once. Peter called, "Curtain time!"

Meg asked Elly, "You're coming to the performance?"

"Of course."

"If you want to come wiv' me now, I can show you 'round before 'alf 'our. You'll be in our dressing room."

Rory rolled his eyes. "Won't that be a treat."

Chapter 3

Jeremy O'Connell had not moved since his head plunged into the pillow on his dressing-room cot. He could have slept through the night. There was a sharp rap on the door and, "Six o'clock Mr. O'Connell, 'eres your tea." In walked Timmy the pub-boy, gracefully balancing a large covered tray on one hand.

Mouth-watering aromas made Jeremy sit up. "So, Timmy, with what is your good mother bewitching me tonight?"

Timmy pondered the question. He was a slight lad, aged twenty who looked fourteen. A smile came over his face. "Oh, 'at's funny sir, 'bewitchin' like i' *Macbeth*." He laughed at his own cleverness.

Jeremy screamed, "The Scottish Play!" closed his eyes and fought to control his temper. Remembering that this was dull little Timmy and not one of his sharp-witted actors, his words became soft and deliberate. "Timmy, we - do - not - speak - the - name - of - this - play. We have discussed this. You remember, do you not?"

In absolute horror, Timmy's hand went to his mouth. His cheeks glowed bright red. "U'mm sorry, sir. So sorry." He dashed from the dressing-room, slamming the door behind him.

Jeremy counted, "One, two, three, four, five, six, seven."

The door burst open. Timmy was flushed and panting. "Oi turned around three times and swore an oath. 'at's right, weren't it sir? Just the way you taught me."

"I am sure that was sufficient, Timmy. All the bad luck has gone away. Thank you for bringing the tea, goodbye."

At exactly six-thirty, a disembodied hand, holding a dark wig on a stand, floated through Jeremy's open door. The head moved in rhythm to a high singsong, "Have you heard, my pretty King?" Eugene the wig-master popped his top half around the door, leaving his legs in the hall. He fluttered with delight.

Jeremy enjoyed Eugene's foppish antics. "And what, pray tell, should I have heard?"

"The entire run of The Scottish Play is sold out. The public is lined around the building clamouring for tickets. They are killing each other to see *you*, my liege. Ooh!" Eugene squealed with delight, danced in on tiptoe, and genuflected, presenting the wig head as an offering.

"The entire run. Are you sure?" Now, he was deadly serious.

"Yes, yes. I was just downstairs in the box office."

"But this is thrilling. Not since Simon Camden's *Hamlet* has a play sold out after the first night. What a triumph. What a victory." Jeremy nodded grandly. "Sirrah, my thanks."

"My most noble majesty." Eugene placed the wig-head on the dressing table, bowed low, and backed out, straight into Jeremy's one-time lover, Tommy Quinn. Eugene batted his long dark eyelashes and pranced on his way. Tommy enjoyed the adoration, but stayed where he was.

Jeremy scowled. "I wasn't expecting you for another week. You're looking very well. New suit?" He turned his back, knocked his pipe against the wastebasket, and emptied the old tobacco.

Tommy sauntered into the room, waved his spotless kid gloves, then eased into Jeremy's chair. "I actually had trouble getting through your crowd of admirers. The stage-doorkeeper didn't want to let me back."

Tommy's hair was freshly trimmed and his clothes immaculate. At thirty-nine, he had lost his boyish good looks. Dark circles framed his bloodshot eyes. Weak arms hung from thin shoulders. The corners of his mouth were heavily lined, and his pleasing smile was spoiled by a missing tooth. He was younger than Jeremy, but looked older.

Jeremy automatically took out his wallet. "How much do you need?"

"Actually, I am here to give some back. After all these years, I must owe you a king's ransom." Playing magician, he wiggled his fingers and pulled a twenty-pound-note from his sleeve. The broad, thin white paper fluttered like a handkerchief.

Jeremy's eyes widened. "This is a surprise. Your pub must be doing well. Who would have guessed it? All your other schemes failed before you even…"

"My other schemes were strictly for survival." He leaned back, admiring the sheer white paper currency flickering between his fingers. "This one is a splendid adventure."

Jeremy looked doubtful. "An adventure? The pub owners I know spend their nights scrubbing glasses, stacking crates, and hauling ruffians into the street."

"Amongst the clientele at *The Pink Kitten*, there are very few ruffians." Tommy pursed his lips and Jeremy sneered.

"It's become a hideaway for Nancy Boys, has it?"

"Let us say, a haven."

Wondering why Tommy was really here, Jeremy pretended to straighten his already pristine dressing-table.

Tommy carefully rolled the twenty pound note into a thin cylinder. "You may remember my telling you about the upstairs rooms."

"Wool storage or something. You said they were filthy and the roof leaked--a waste of space."

"They are not being wasted anymore." He giggled, and a chill ran up Jeremy's spine. "Some of my clientele, especially the married ones, have a devil of a time finding private space where they won't be disturbed. So I repaired the roof and festooned one of those rooms, all pale-blue and lacy, and started renting it by the hour."

Jeremy's stomach soured. "And where, pray tell, were you able to get the financing? I have not been giving you enough for…"

"Archie, of course."

"Archibald Perry?" Jeremy spun around in a fury. "That slime journalist…"

Tommy shrugged. "As you said, you haven't been giving me enough…" he held up his hand, "…not that I am not grateful. You have kept me alive all these years."

"I thought you were looking for theatre work."

"I still make the rounds, fool that I am. No one will hire me."

"Simon Camden will hire you."

"He won't, actually." His smile vanished and an embarrassed flush darkened his cheeks. "Not since I deserted him in the tropics. That tour was bloody hell. We all fell ill with dysentery, malaria, and worse. I'll never complain about foggy England again."

"Last we heard, Simon was in New York. I'd like to tour there, myself."

Shaken, but trying not to show it, Tommy playfully blew through the twenty-pound cylinder. "No, really. He will not hire me. I wrote him a few months ago. I actually begged him. He actually bothered to answer. He wrote two words: 'Never - again.'" Tommy flipped the cylinder open and offered it to Jeremy.

That note was payment from the devil and Jeremy lurched away as if it were spewing flames. "Keep your money, Tommy. I am pleased you are doing well." The small desk clock read six-forty-five. It was nearly half-hour. The other actors would arrive at any moment. He had to get rid of Tommy.

Oblivious to Jeremy's mood, Tommy continued toying with the twenty-pound-note. "I now have four upstairs rooms, busy all hours of the day and night. Had to hire a boy, just to clean and change the sheets. Then, one of my clients took a shine to the boy, and the clever lad discovered he could do ever so much better lying between the sheets than scrubbing them." He chuckled at Jeremy's grimace. "So, old tart, I've got four lucky laddies, working all hours. They used to work the streets for pennies. Now they are well fed, dressed like little gentlemen, and…"

"Have you entirely lost your mind?"

"I told you it was an adventure."

Jeremy slammed the door. Blood pounded in his head. Heart racing, he whispered frantically, "If you end up back in Reading Gaol, will that be an adventure? If they kill you on that sodding treadmill, will that be an adventure? If one of your randy clients decides to slash one of your pretty boys, and you go to the gallows as an accomplice, will that be an adventure?"

"Daddy. Daddy." Softly from a distance, then louder as he sped down the hall, the voice of nine-year-old Evan O'Connell piped, "Daddy, have you seen…?"

Jeremy turned away from Tommy, spitting out a furious, "Get out of here, now." He opened the door, and caught Evan as the boy leapt into his arms.

"Daddy!" His words tumbled all at once. "Have you seen the crowds outside? Mummy could barely get through all the people wanted her autograph to touch her and talk to her isn't it exciting?"

"Yes, Evan, it is exciting."

Tommy stood in the doorway, smiling benignly. "Evan love, got a kiss for your Uncle Tommy?" Hands behind his back, he coquettishly offered his cheek. The backstage area was filling with actors and technicians.

Jeremy had to avoid a scene. Reluctantly, he put Evan down, and smiled when the boy backed away from Tommy.

Evan's mother, actress Katherine Stewart, arrived in time to see Tommy straighten up. "Hello Kathy. You're looking ravishing, as always. Congratulations on The Scottish Play." He stroked Evan's blond hair. "He's such a sweet boy. Boys can be so very useful. 'Bye all. Have a good show." He pocketed his twenty-pound-note, smiled smugly, and sauntered away.

Katherine and Jeremy looked uneasy as they watched Tommy cross the stage and leave the theatre. Long ago, Jeremy had loved Tommy. They had been very happy together. Jeremy missed those gay days and wondered why they had gone so terribly wrong. Suddenly afraid of losing the family he now held dear, he kept one hand on Evan's shoulder, clutched Katherine around the waist and kissed her hard. He wished they could stay like that forever. He only let Katherine go after she gave him a playful push, and winked at Evan.

Jeremy sighed happily. "Sold-out Katie. Did you hear?"

"Yes. Isn't it marvelous?"

He pulled Evan closer. "And it's all because of you, Young Macduff."

Katherine trilled a laugh. "Yes darling. You were brilliant. And -- we do it again, within the hour." She glided across the stage to her dressing-room. After fourteen years together, Jeremy still loved watching her. At thirty-four, her dancer's body retained its youthful grace. There was no sound as her feet lightly skimmed the floorboards.

Chapter 4

Apprentice actors Rory, Lester, and Todd raced each other out of the boardinghouse door, pulling on coats and mufflers as they went. Living only minutes from the theatre, they seldom bothered to button up. Tonight, icy wind stung like needles in their faces and hands. Todd's long, rubber-like limbs swung from side to side. He bumped Rory off the narrow sidewalk, dangerously close to a carriage. The horse shied and the driver swore.

Rory was furious. "Keep your bloody arms to yourself, can't you. You're a walking disaster." He put his head down, shoved his hands in his pockets, and charged into the wind, pulling ahead of the other two. His thick blond hair blew in every direction.

Todd continued flapping in the wind. "Miss Fielding's gorgeous! Absolutely gorgeous!"

Lester's coat hung open, framing his belly, as he sped past Todd to reach Rory. Running sideways, keeping his round face close to Rory's, he shouted into the wind. "She has such a sweet face. Did you see how upset she was during your row with Peg? I thought she was going to faint." He shivered and finally pulled his coat closed. "I wonder if she's ever heard that kind of language?" Rory plowed ahead, wishing Lester would leave him alone.

"She's so gorgeous!" Todd chanted, his long body swaying almost in a dance.

Lester persisted. "She barely ate anything. Of course Peg had stolen most of her share before she even got to table. She looked so frightened." He chuckled and shook his head. "I feel so sorry for her. I don't know how she's going to live with Meg and Peg. Of course, after your scene, we probably won't see Peg for a while."

Rory was fuming. "Shut up, will you!" He raced even faster.

Lester was ecstatic. His favorite sport was teasing Rory, and he had never done it quite this well. An evil grin crossed his face as he ran to catch up. "Why in hell does Peg still love you? Do all the girls you shag fall in love with you? Why don't you fall in love for a change… and get dropped… and take some of your own medicine? I know! Why don't you fall in love with Miss Fielding?"

"She's so gorgeous!" Todd gurgled, now running as well, his long arms flapping like wings. "I'm in love with her and I don't even like girls." He laughed hysterically.

Rory spun around. "Why don't you both shut up! Bloody stupid sods! What do you know about it? What do you know about me? What makes you think I never fall in love?"

Lester reached up and pulled Todd's head down into a conspirator's pose. "Todd, old boy, do you see what I see?" He pointed to Rory. "I think our friend has fallen in love, practically at first sight, too. What do you think of that then?" They were almost at the stage door. Rory glared, bit his thumb at them, pushed through the crowd of autograph seekers, and ran inside. Lester put his hand over his heart and pretended to be shocked. "Did he bite his thumb at us, sir?"

Todd recited back, "No sir, but he did bite his thumb, sir."

*

Unlike the raucous boys, Meg acted very superior, leading Elly to the theatre. The stage door was blocked by a crowd of patrons. Meg made a hugely theatrical gesture, and shouted with a piercing voice, " 'scuse us very kindly, we 'ave to get ready fo' the performance."

Inside, a different stage-doorkeeper sat at the high desk. He was a younger man. "Good evening Miss O'Mally, Miss Fielding." He held out his hand. "I'm Alberts."

Elly shook his hand. "How-do-you-do, Mr. Alberts? It's so nice to meet you." Her smile was sweet and Alberts looked enchanted.

"Welcome to 'is Majesty's."

"Come along now, Elly," Meg's tone was condescending. "We must ge' a move on. I 'ave a performance tonight."

"I'm so sorry." Elly spoke with appropriate deference. Alberts chuckled, giving her an understanding wink. Elly smiled at Mr. Alberts, blushed slightly, and followed Meg through a corridor and down a staircase taking them under the stage.

Michael had been wrong about one thing, Elly had power. Her physical beauty, unaffected charm, and simple good manners were winning her conquests at every turn.

Meg stood close and whispered. "I always take a wash before the show. The washrooms is this way."

Inside the women's washroom, Elly was delighted to find a large tub of water warming on a gas stove. It was filled from a single tap, sticking out of the wall. The slate floor sloped down to a drain in the center. Tin basins were stacked on a wide ledge. A row of worn but clean towels hung over a clothesline and cakes of soap lay in a saucer. A large drying rack was filled with ladies' clothing.

Elly asked, "Can I do my washing here?"

Meg filled one of the tin basins and set it on the ledge. "We do all our washin' 'ere. There's no water at Potter's."

Elly filled a basin and washed her hands and face.

Meg washed only her hands. "I wash m' face after the show, when I take m' makeup off."

From the look of her skin, Elly wondered if Meg ever took off her makeup. Most of the dark greasepaint seemed to be smeared across the bed sheets at the boarding house.

Meg led the way back upstairs to the stage level. The wing space at the side of the stage was painted white. The floors were smooth, unvarnished wood. She pointed to a dressing room with the number 2 on the door.

"This is the quick-change room. Our dressing room's upstairs but we change down 'ere when there's no time to go all the way up and down again."

The next door, number 4, had a polished brass name plate with MISS STEWART engraved in beautiful script. Elly smiled to herself, remembering Mrs. Potter's boardinghouse doors. Meg whispered, "It's not 'alf-hour yet, but 'er door is closed so we won't disturb Miss Stewart. I'll introduce you later. Come on, let's go over t' the other side."

They walked onto the stage, brightly lit and full of scenery. Unhurried scene-shifters placed fake looking bushes and trees onto marks painted on the floor. A backdrop featured a toy castle set against roughly painted dark streaks. It hung loose and waved slightly as the girls walked by. Two men carried a large black cauldron. They used only one hand each and it appeared to weigh very little. After carefully setting it on its marks, they went to tie down the backdrop.

Stage-manager Eddy Edwards walked to his desk down-stage left, and waved a greeting to the girls.

He shouted, "Heads up, curtain coming down!"

Off to stage right, a well-muscled man reached up with two hands and pulled on a thick rope running from floor to ceiling. Elly was thrilled to see the heavy red-and-gold curtain slowly descend, until its huge weight made a muffled *whoosh* against the wooden floor. She recognized the large stage-right wing where she and the other hopefuls had waited to audition. The empty dressing room 1, where Michael had helped her prepare, was now another quick-change room, full of velvet and brocade costumes dyed rich earth tones: browns, dark-reds, and dark greens.

The next door, 3, was half-open. The brass name plate read MR. O'CONNELL. Elly saw the name, caught her breath, and stepped back.

*

The clatter of hard-soled shoes and rowdy voices announced the arrival of two-dozen actors for their half-hour call. Jeremy O'Connell chuckled to see his ratty band of apprentices straggle in. Meg and the new girl came straight towards him. Meg's small feet supported heavy legs, a thick body, and a large head topped-off with an enormous hat. The total design made her an almost perfect kite. The new girl looked slim and charmingly plain by comparison. The hem of her pale-green frock was mud spattered under her schoolgirl coat. Her radiant hair was tied back under a modest wool bonnet.

Meg pushed open the door with a theatrical, "Good evening', Mr. O'Connell."

Jeremy's rich theatrical tones mimicked her pretentious grandeur. "A very good evening to you, Miss O'Mally."

Meg whispered, "Say 'ello," gave Elly a push, and watched as she awkwardly fell into the room.

Regaining her balance, Elly looked at Jeremy O'Connell and blinked with surprise.

He sat in a richly upholstered chair, dressed in a hand-painted silk dressing-gown. His eyes were clear, his dark hair was combed back, and one manicured finger touched his thin lips. His street clothes and costumes hung on a neat rack. An oriental rug covered the floor and heavy green drapes swayed against a partially opened window. Two carved wooden chairs and a narrow cot filled most of the space. Gilt mirrors, framed photos, and letters covered the walls. Even his stove was polished. His dressing table held perfect rows of grease sticks, charcoal pencils, and fake hair for mustaches and beards. It was a tiny jewel of a room.

Elly stood very still, her hands clutched together.

Jeremy was sure the other apprentices had frightened her with tales of his often sadistic nature. He studied her as if she were a laboratory rat.

"Ah yes, Miss..." He stopped, thought for a moment, remembered the name Round-tree, and shook his head. "We changed your name, did we not?" She started to speak, but he held up a hand. "No, no, wait. Let me think... El... Elly. Yes?" She nodded. He held up his hand again. "El-ly-Fiel-ding." He almost sang the name, separating the syllables.

She stammered, "Y' Yes sir."

"You see, I was not quite as hung-over as you thought I was." His manner was so broadly theatrical, he wondered if she knew he was only teasing.

Her cheeks flushed. Tears filled her eyes. "I beg your pardon sir, I thought nothing at all."

"Nothing at all? Only a salamander thinks nothing at all."

Her eyes bulged, and he guessed she had been warned never to disagree with him. He softened his tone. "It is I who should beg your pardon. This afternoon, I presented myself as less than a gentleman." His voice dropped low. "Forgive me."

Elly looked totally confused. She started to answer back, stopped herself, and stared at the floor. Her self-control was marvellous. He hoped that he could harness her energy and teach her to use her beauty. She could be a sensation. He would make her into an actress.

He fluttered a hand. "I can see you are in the very capable hands of Miss O'Mally. Please enjoy the play, come back after, and tell me what you think."

"Thank you, sir. I look forward to this evening. I have not had the pleasure of seeing you on stage since you played Skipton."

"Skipton? But... that must have been..."

She laughed appealingly. "Yes sir, I was a child, but I remember you very well. You were Henry the Fifth, and I fell in love."

Overpowered by her flattery, he smiled in spite of himself, then quickly turned away. "Goodbye."

*

34

Meg led Elly up the stairs, shaking her head. "Can't believe wha' O'Connell just said. 'at's a first. Never 'eard 'at ol' pouf say 'beg pardon' to the likes of us."

Elly asked, "What's a pouf?"

"A Jessie."

"What's a Jessie?"

Meg made a face. "You know, a Nancy Boy."

Elly shook her head, still not understanding.

Meg stared at her in disbelief. "Good God, almighty!" She continued up the stairs.

Up one flight were two dressing rooms, 5 and 7, with four men in each. Meg made the introductions. "Chaps, this is Elly. Elly, this 'ere's room five. 'ere's Kenny, Ollie, Owen, and Evan. Back 'ere', in room seven, you've got Brian, George, Donald, and you know Michael. You'll 'ave to remember the rooms when yer workin' in the costume shop."

The actors greeted her warmly.

Michael led Elly onto the landing. "Are you all right? I feel terrible. I left you on the street. I'm so sorry."

So much in the past few hours had been new and unpleasant, Michael's sweet words almost made her cry. "Oh Mr. Burns – Michael, you were so tired and you've been so kind to me. I'm fine, everything's fine, really." Tears burst from her eyes and streamed down her cheeks.

He handed her a handkerchief and she blew her nose. He whispered, "I told you Potter's was a beastly place."

"It is, but I'll survive. Truly! I'm not as fragile as I look."

He raised an eyebrow. "I hope that's true."

Meg commanded, "Come along, Elly."

She held the handkerchief to her heart. "Let me wash this for you."

"If you like." Michael gave her his most encouraging smile.

She smiled back, clutched the handkerchief for support, then followed Meg to the top floor. They were greeted by their male housemates and a host of other men. Lester, Todd, Rory, and Peter shared one room. Ten supernumeraries were crammed into the other. Since there were only four chairs, they took turns applying their makeup, then waiting in the hall. Elly was reminded that Shakespeare wrote many roles for men, but few for women. She noted the room numbers: 9 and 11.

When Rory saw Elly, he dropped his makeup sponge and leapt from his chair. One of his cheeks was dark with greasepaint, and he looked like a little boy with a dirty face. Elly smiled in spite of herself.

Meg took off, up a very steep, narrow staircase. Elly followed and Rory raced after them, taking Elly's arm. "Mind your step now. It's a bit tricky up here."

Meg sneered, "'It's a bit tricky up 'ere.' I been 'ere two years, Rory, an' y' never walked me up them stairs."

Elly was determined to stop this row before it started. "Oh, Miss O'Mally, you're so good at so many things, and I have such a lot to learn. I'm sure Mr. Cook is only worried I'll break my silly neck."

Meg accepted this with a sarcastic, "Right!" She entered dressing room 10. It was occupied by the two lady apprentices.

Peg was finishing her Second Witch makeup. The point of her razor-sharp chin extended into impossibly thin cheeks and huge eyes in ghostly sockets. She snarled at Elly, "Wha' in 'ell you doin' 'ere?"

Elly gasped and stepped back.

Rory raced to defend. "She's got as much right to be in here as you lot, and you'd better get used to her being…"

"Mr. Cook, please!" Elly glared, begging him to be quiet. Very deliberately she turned back to Peg. "Miss O'Mally has been kind enough to show me around, Miss. Lamoor. I shall now go into the stalls where I belong. I beg your pardon for the intrusion. I look forward to your performance." She smiled at the scowling witch face, turned her back, and shuddered.

The call-boy shouted from two floors below. "'alf hour, laidies!" He saw Rory, "and gen'leman."

Rory stammered, "I'll just run Miss Fielding down to the stalls."

"Make it quick. Don't let the gov' see you."

"Come on, Elly." They hurried down the stairs.

She stopped him half-way. "Mr. Cook, promise me something."

He spun around, almost knocking her over. "Yes, of course, anything in the world."

She backed away from him. "I have to live with Meg and Peg. Please don't make them hate me."

"Right." He looked ashamed of himself. "Sorry."

They continued down the stairs and she stopped him again. "There's one thing more."

"Anything. Just ask."

"Well, Jeremy O'Connell said I should come back after the performance. Do you suppose he meant it?"

"Absolutely. If he asked you to come back, you must do it." He left her and sped back upstairs.

Elly put her wool cap in her pocket, took off her coat and folded it over her arm. She shook out her skirt and her hair, hoping she looked presentable. She opened a door leading from the dim backstage area, into a curtained vestibule, pushed the curtain aside, and stepped into the brightly lit stalls. The pit orchestra played lively music; loud enough to be heard, but not interrupt the cheerful conversations of elegantly dressed ladies and gentlemen, squeezing past each other, finding their seats.

All the men wore black-and-white dress suits. The women paraded in colourful beaded gowns, silks, furs and jewels. The excitement was electric. Crystal chandeliers beamed sparkling light. The seats were upholstered plush red with gold trim, matching the red-and-gold of the stage curtain. Gilded carvings of cherubs playing musical instruments, and murals of Greek lovers were everywhere.

An elegant lady noticed Elly's soiled frock, turned to her woman friend, and spoke loudly. "I don't know what *my* maids do on their nights off, but I certainly wouldn't want to see one of them here."

An usher hurried to her. "Gallery stairs are at the back, Miss. Got a ticket?"

Elly's cheeks flushed with embarrassment. "No, I haven't. I'm a new apprentice. Mr. Bates said…"

The usher's scowl relaxed into a smile. "Oh, *you're* the one. Right-i-o. We're sold out, cha know, even standing room. You'll have to watch from the back wiv' us. Seats usually get freed-up second act. I'll keep m' eye out fer y'. They call me Old Jim, on a count a there's a lad 'ere, and 'e's…"

"Young Jim?" Elly finished and they both laughed. "Thanks, Old Jim, you're very kind. I'm Elly." She smiled and offered her hand.

Old Jim shook her lovely hand, smiled back, and fancied himself in love. He led Elly to the back of the stalls and introduced her to the other ushers. The houselights began to dim.

Jeremy O'Connell looked in his dressing-room mirror. Macbeth looked back. Greasepaint and charcoal sharpened his delicate features. Dark auburn wig hair was combed back over his shoulders, and a slender beard framed his chin. He was Macbeth -- a warrior, a patriot, a weak-willed murderer.

Glancing across his dressing-table, he smiled at a family photograph of Katherine, Evan, and himself on a pebble beach. Beside it stood a photo of a handsome young man, holding a violin. He whispered, "Stephen, my pretty boy, I hope you are not having too much fun on tour." He chuckled sadly. "I miss you, you little tart."

A boy's voice called, "Five minutes, Mr. O'Connell."

"Thank you, Matt."

Backstage was a beehive of activity. Jeremy walked over to Katherine. Her face was painted sharp and dark. Thick red wig-hair fell to her waist. He took her hand and raised it to his lips.

Eddie called, "Ladies and gentlemen, beginners for Act One. Places please!"

The houselights dimmed and the audience ceased their chatter. The house went to black and eerie music sounded from violins playing close harmonies in their highest registers. Double basses bowed their lowest open strings. The curtain rose and Elly's heart pounded. The stage she had walked across was now the Scottish moors. A real castle stood in the distance and a real storm was raging.

Downstage-right, Peg McCarthy and two older actresses appeared as three terrifying witches, stirring a fiercely bubbling caldron. Behind them, a dozen ghostly figures converged in the shadows.

Stage-right disappeared into darkness, and stage-left blazed with cold blue light. A dozen soldiers wielded huge metal swords that clashed together, launching a mighty battle. The music surged as the stage filled with a dozen more soldiers swinging axes and shields. Women in the audience gasped and fluttered their fans.

Owen Freeman, dark and handsome, entered as Malcolm. Michael Burns, fair and lithe, entered as Ross. Some soldiers howled with victory. Others shrieked with pain. Todd, dressed in gleaming chain mail, strode downstage, then viciously hurled his ax upstage. Lester and another soldier held up their shields, stopping the ax with a terrible crash. Rory

Cook raised his sword over his head and drove it into Todd's side. The Witches reappeared in the mist.

A drum roll — a great flash of lightning — and Jeremy O'Connell stood center-stage — tall, dark, and magnificent, a huge broadsword rested on his shoulder. His voice cut through the storm. "*So foul and fair a day I have not seen.*" A swift lift of his head brought the witches swarming around him. An excited hum rose from the audience. He was Macbeth—a sinewy, well-muscled warrior with no thoughts other than serving his king and his personal ambition. A hard man, yet still a likable man, vulnerable and self-doubting.

The scene changed to inside the castle walls. Oddly sweet music brought Lady Macbeth gliding onto the stage. Katherine Stewart was fascinating, mysterious, and sensual. Her beauty would be Macbeth's undoing. Rory Cook appeared in small roles, always intense and forceful.

The interval came and the audience poured into lounge areas for refreshments. Elly wandered into the lobby. Large framed photographs of actors lined the walls. Jeremy O'Connell's company hung on one side, and Herbert Beerbohm Tree's touring company on the other. All the actors had been photographed in wonderfully melodramatic poses. Jeremy O'Connell's picture hung first. The next picture was… Elly stopped. She read the name a second time. There had to a mistake. This could not be Katherine Stewart, the actress playing Lady Macbeth. The woman in the picture was blond with a sweet, beautiful face. Suddenly, Elly remembered Jeremy O'Connell's dark wig and Peg's witch makeup. These were real actors, not children in a school play.

The next pictures were the men she had met backstage, and a few women she had not met. Little Evan was there. She read his name, *Evan O'Connell*. He looked exactly like Katherine Stewart. Miss Stewart and Mr. O'Connell must be his parents.

*

During the intermission, cast and crew prepared for the second act. It took Jeremy O'Connell only minutes to change his tunic, comb his wig, and freshen his makeup. When his dresser took his first act tunic away, Jeremy saw Rory Cook hover nervously near the door. Whatever did he want?

"Mr. Cook?"

"Mr. O'Connell, sir."

"Won't you come in?" Jeremy adored Rory, was prepared to give him anything, but would have good sport making him work for it. He offered Rory a chair, then sat down and crossed his legs. "You appear to have come on a mission, Mr. Cook. What can I do for you?"

Rory leapt up, stammering, "Well sir... you see sir... it's like this sir." Sweat gleamed through his makeup. He glanced through the open doorway. "May we speak privately, sir?"

"Of course, my boy." Now, Jeremy was concerned.

Rory closed the door, pulled a chair close, and spoke in hushed tones. "You see sir, there's a new apprentice, a lovely girl, she..."

"Miss Fielding."

"Yes sir... you see, sir... she's lovely."

"So you said."

"Yes, sir. She is nothing like the others."

"Nothing like the others." What did he want, a love potion?

"She's well-bred and educated, and, well... she's a lady."

"Yes." Jeremy nodded seriously. "All right. So far I'm with you." This was funny.

"Well sir, she... she..."

"Yes?"

"She's new here, and she's not had much experience."

"No."

"On the stage, that is."

"No."

"She'll be in your class. You'll try to teach her... I mean you *will* teach her. You're a brilliant teacher." There was a knock on the door. "Damn!" Rory drove a fist into his open palm.

A boy's voice called, "Five minutes, Mr. O'Connell."

"Thank you, Matt."

"She doesn't like me." He buried his head in his hands.

"What?"

"She doesn't like me. Everything I say is wrong. She won't even talk to me."

"How is this possible? She only arrived a few hours ago."

"Well sir, it was at tea, at Mrs. Potter's. We're always a bit rough there. I hadn't even seen that she was at the table, and..." He closed his eyes, raised his chin and looked as if he were about to cry.

Jeremy threw up his hands. "All right laddie, tell me what happened, but quickly."

Rory took a deep breath and raced through his story.

Jeremy shook his head. "My dear boy, I see the ghastly picture all too clearly. However, a mere quarter-hour after that disastrous tea, Elly Fielding was in my dressing-room appearing none the worse for wear. My guess is that she was less distressed than you imagined. Perhaps she has come from a chaotic household and is used to rowdy behaviour. We must never assume that a lady's outward appearance reveals her inner mettle."

The call-boy knocked on the door. "Places, Mr. O'Connell."

"Thank God." He hurried out with Rory at his heels. "So, what in the world do you want from me?"

"Please sir, give us a scene together, then she'll have to talk to me."

Jeremy nearly tripped over his own feet. This was hilarious, but he pretended to be shocked. He glared down at Rory. "Give you a scene together. Are you serious?" Rory's sweet eyes pleaded and Jeremy was tempted to give in to him, then and there. He fluttered a hand. "It is too late now. Go on stage, boy. Talk to me after. I need to think."

When the final curtain fell, the audience was on its feet. Women sobbed into handkerchiefs. Men cheered. The ovation went on and on. When the cheering finally stopped, the stage curtain lowered and stayed still.

Jeremy sat in front of his dressing-table, using lard and a rag to wipe off his makeup. He felt very calm and almost meditative as he meticulously went over every inch of his face and neck.

In the corner of his mirror, he could see Elly Fielding standing in the hallway. She saw his smiling reflection. He spoke into the mirror, "Won't you come in, my dear," and gestured toward a chair.

"Thank you, sir." Smiling shyly, she walked in and sat down.

His posture was easy. "So, what did you think of our Scottish Play?"

She looked very serious. "Well, sir, I had read the play but never seen it. On paper Macbeth seems a feeble-minded murderer and I never felt the slightest sympathy." She looked him straight in the eye. "You made me care about you. I felt sorry for you. I wanted to hate you, but I could not." Her voice rose with each excited line. "I did not want you to die. You did not want to kill anyone. It was not your fault. I hated Lady

Macbeth for seducing you into it. She was so evil I wanted to kill her."
She lowered her eyes, nervously waiting for his response.

He chuckled softly. "Thank you. I think that is my favourite review to date."

"Daddy!" Evan flew into the room. "It was wonderful. No terrible second night for us."

"No laddie, not for us. We *were* wonderful." He gave the boy a hug.

Evan beamed. "Hello Miss Fielding, did you like the play?"

"You were marvelous. I was so sad when you died."

"Dying is fun. I never got to die before. I died in *Richard the Third*, but that was offstage. No one saw it."

She nodded in sympathy. "Why would a second night be terrible?"

Proud to be the authority, Evan explained, "Well, you see, opening nights are usually fine, because everyone is nervous and keyed up. Second night, everyone relaxes, and some make stupid blunders. The Scottish Play is especially dangerous, because bad things have happened during other productions." He leaned on Jeremy. "Mummy said not to wait for her, so I'm going to the pub. Are you having supper tonight?"

"Yes, why not? Miss Fielding, do us the honour of joining two unworthy gentlemen for a light repast."

Elly gasped with surprise. "Thank you, sir. I would be delighted."

Evan saw Jeremy's used supper tray, pulled off the serviette and smiled to find scraps of crust and chicken gravy. "No, Evan." Jeremy rolled my eyes. "The cats do not need that tiny bit of nourishment. They have plenty of mice." Evan seized the plate and flew up the stairs. Elly watched with a puzzled look, as Jeremy shrugged and slipped on his coat. "Evan is sure the theatre cats will perish without his offerings."

She smiled in surprise. "I haven't seen any cats."

"Nor will you, unless you are walking the cat-walk." He chuckled at his play-on-words. "It is dangerous and you should never have occasion to cross that precariously high and narrow roadway that serves as a bridge between stage-right and left. Come, let us be on our way." Elly followed him into the hall.

He locked his dressing-room door as Rory charged across the stage. "Mr. O'Connell, I'm late, forgive me," he panted, "I was delayed by a wardrobe difficulty. I am so glad you're still here." He stopped dead when he saw Elly. His face was still coated with a thin film of dark paint. His hands were filthy and his hair needed combing.

Jeremy chuckled, "Join us for supper, Mr. Cook?" Elly smiled shyly and Rory beamed.

"Thank you, sir." He noticed his hands. "Just give me a minute to wash. I'll join you in the pub."

As Jeremy and Elly crossed the stage, he pointed up to the cat-walk and Evan balancing on two narrow planks. "Those cats are feral and seldom come near humans. We need them to control the mice, and every theatre has cats. Without them, mice chew holes through scenery, but worse, they gnaw through ropes, sometimes causing fatal accidents. I believe that half the world's theatre ghosts are actually cats."

Elly caught her breath. "Does this theatre have a ghost?"

"No, it's too new. The first production was only in 1897. No one has had a chance to die here, yet." She blinked, but said nothing. Todd and Lester appeared as if by magic. Jeremy often fed his starving apprentices. He chuckled at their perfect timing. "Join us for supper, lads?"

They chanted in chorus. "Yes, sir. Thank you, sir."

The Actress and Villain was already crowded with good humoured actors, backstage crew, their families and friends. The dreaded second night of the cursed Scottish Play had ended without incident. Tomorrow was a daytime day off. Everyone was happy and relaxed, eating, drinking, and joking. Jeremy inhaled the pleasant aroma of hot food and waved to Timmy behind the long service bar.

Lester took Elly's arm. "Here y' are, m' lovely." He pulled out a chair for her and quickly crammed himself into the chair at her right. Rory shoved Todd aside and slid into the chair on Elly's left. Jeremy chuckled and sat across, with Todd and Evan on either side of him. Soon the young actors were helping themselves from bowls of mutton stew, chicken pie, bangers and mash, bread, potatoes, mushy peas, pickled onions, pints of beer and lemonade. Jeremy picked from the dishes and enjoyed watching the famished young people clean their plates. Lester kept Elly giggling with silly jokes. Every time Rory spoke or reached for something, Elly shied away.

"Here's Mummy!" Evan sat up, watching Katherine Stewart squeeze through the noisy crowd. Her fair skin glowed and her thick blond hair was tied back with a ribbon. They all stood.

"Please, don't bother." She motioned for them to sit, moved behind her son's chair, and kissed the top of his head.

Jeremy took her hand and held it to his cheek. "Katie, I do not think you have met our new apprentice, Elly Fielding."

Elly maneuvered around the table. She stooped slightly, surprised to find that she was taller than Katherine.

"I'm so pleased to meet you, Miss Fielding. You'll be a lovely addition to our stable." Katherine offered her hand and smiled warmly.

Elly's eyes widened as she shook Katherine's hand. "Stable, ma'am?"

Katherine laughed. "Just an old expression. We're all like horses under one roof."

"Oh, I see." As Elly's smile broadened, a charming blush coloured her cheeks.

Katherine raised an eyebrow. "She's beautiful, Jerry. You did well. Where did you find her?"

"Michael Burns found her, actually. The credit goes to him. I don't know where she came from. That is still a mystery."

Elly stared at him, then the floor. She suddenly looked afraid.

Eric Bates pushed through the crowd, smiled and waved. Elly slithered back to her seat as Rory grimaced, whispering, "Here comes the good father."

Jeremy glared at him.

"Uncle Eric!" Evan ran in front of Katherine, blocking Eric's path. "Holly and Beth invited me for the puppet show and ice cream, but Mummy said that I must ask Mrs. Bates if it's all right"

Eric shrugged. "Of course, dear boy. Mrs. Bates handles the girls' social engagements. You will have to ask her." He moved Evan gently aside and continued toward Katherine. She glanced over his shoulder and signalled a warning. Eric spun around and saw his wife standing in the doorway, holding a ledger book and glaring through the crowd.

Jeremy had known Hilda Bates for a dozen years. Her grim expression and colourless wardrobe reminded him of an evil school mistress. Her hair was always tied back and her face scrubbed clean. Hilda loathed Katherine and Evan, barely tolerated Jeremy, but was the financial brain of their theatre company. Eric took the credit, but everyone knew Hilda's management kept them afloat. Occasionally, she joined members of the company for a meal. Tonight she would not. Eric shrugged sadly and plodded wearily back.

Evan boldly darted through the obstacle course of chairs and people, straight up to the scowling Hilda. "Mrs. Bates, Holly and Beth invited me for the puppet show and ice cream, but..." Snubbing him completely, Hilda turned on her heel and left the pub.

Evan came back to Katherine and hung his head. "I tried, Mummy."

"You did very well, darling. Better ask her tomorrow. She'll be less cross after she's totaled the receipts." Like a dejected puppy, Evan slowly climbed back onto his chair.

Jeremy stood and offered his chair. "Sit down, Katie. I'll find another." As he slid past her, their familiar bodies rubbed against each other. She kissed his cheek in passing. He managed another step, then stopped when he saw actor Owen Freeman, dark and handsome, sail through the door, thrusting his way toward Katherine.

When she turned her back on Owen, pursing her lips in distaste, Jeremy quietly scolded, "Now, now, Katie, be a good girl. Since the poor chap pleases you so well between the sheets, the least you can do is listen to his intellectual drivel over a glass of wine."

Katherine stifled a laugh. "I love you, Jerry." She squeezed his hand, then smiled at Owen and pushed her way into the next room. Owen politely nodded to Jeremy and followed Katherine.

Evan pointed to the bar, covered with filled glasses. "Timmy needs a hand." He ran to help serve.

Elly asked, "Who are Beth and Holly?

Lester answered, "Mr. Bates's daughters."

Rory snickered, "Evan's sisters."

Jeremy slammed his hand on the table and stared daggers. Whatever Rory felt about Katherine's long-ago affair with Eric Bates, he was not going to voice it in Jeremy's presence.

Chapter 5

By the time Lester, Todd, Elly, Rory, and Jeremy buttoned their coats and left the pub, the air was fresh and frigid. Rory let the other apprentices hurry past.

Jeremy studied the sky. "'*Not from the stars do I my judgment pluck; And yet methinks I have astronomy...*' Forget something, Mr. Cook?"

Shivering, Rory crossed his arms and stamped his feet. "No sir, it's just such a lovely night. I thought I might walk a bit."

Jeremy wondered what Rory wanted this time. "Really? It's bloody cold. Very well, if you must walk, you can walk with me." The streetlights made grotesquely long shadows as they continued up Haymarket.

When they turned onto Panton Street, Rory broke the silence. "Forgive me, sir. I may have spoken out of turn, earlier, but everyone knows about Evan being Mr. Bates's..."

Jeremy tensed, but kept walking.

"If Miss Fielding stays, she's sure to hear of it from someone, so I didn't think it mattered.if I..." Jeremy stared straight ahead and continued walking.

Now, Rory was frantic. "Evan's the most marvelous boy. He's terribly lucky having
you. I wish my father cared a-quarter-as-much for me."

Jeremy glanced sideways.

Encouraged that he had Jeremy's attention, Rory breathlessly continued. "I just think Evan deserves better than a real father who barely tolerates him and a mother who keeps..."

Jeremy spun to face him. "A mother who... What?"

Shocked, Rory's mouth went dry. "Well sir... It is no secret that Miss Stewart has a dozen gentlemen calling every week. Some nights, her dressing-room is a veritable flower shop. She receives lavish gifts, even jewels."

Jeremy spoke without emotion. "She is a great actress with a huge following. Do you find fault with that?"

"Not at all, except that she doesn't care for any of the men who court her."

"And how would you know who she cares for? Are you privy to her private thoughts?"

"No, sir, but I see these men at the stage door. Wealthy, powerful men. Foreigners, sometimes."

"And how often do you see her leave the theatre with these men?"

He stopped to think. "I have never seen her, but she must…"

"You have never seen her, because she refuses all invitations."

"What about Owen Freeman? He's my friend, so I know he loves her -- worships her, in fact. She treats him like a lapdog, petting him one moment, then putting him out for the night."

"Mr. Freeman is a different story altogether." Jeremy picked up his pace.

"But, why does she even bother with him? A blind man can see she only cares for you, and why do you call her Katie? All her other friends call her Kathy. Mr. Bates called her Katie once, she didn't like it."

Jeremy stopped. "The name is no secret. As a child, she was called Kathy. When we first met, I thought the name too compliant. I called her Katie, instead."

"Was that before Evan?"

"Years before Evan."

"But, if she was with you, how could she have been with…"

"Enough questions!" More tired than angry, Jeremy exhaled a cloud of slow mist.

Rory shoved his hands into his pockets and stayed close to Jeremy's side. "Please sir. I respect you both so terribly much. I just want to understand you, to see how you live. I don't really know who you are."

"Few people do." Jeremy walked on and Rory followed.

"I have never known anyone like you, respected anyone the way I respect you, needed the respect of anyone as much as I need yours."

Jeremy stopped short. "You have my total respect; surely you know that, and my affection."

"I know nothing of the kind. Most days you seem to hate me." His voice tightened. "I gave up everything to study with you--my home, my family, my inheritance. You wanted me to stay at Oxford. You told me not to come. It was totally my decision and I'm not sorry. I'd do it again. It's been wonderful."

Jeremy looked down at Rory, exhausted and nearly in tears. "You don't look as though it has been wonderful. I have done my best to make it hell."

"It's been terribly hard. I've never been so tired, or dirty, or hungry, but I've also never been challenged the way you challenge me. You never let me relax." He swallowed the lump in his throat. "You force me to do my best, every moment. I've hated you for it, and I..." He gasped for air. "I love you for it." Cheeks burning, he turned away.

Jeremy took a moment, breathing hard, shaking his head. "Christ, what a shambles." He started to put a comforting hand on Rory's shoulder, thought better of it, and crossed his arms over his chest. "Dear boy, this is the witching hour when ghosts and goblins haunt our souls. It is very late. We are both very tired, and liable to say foolish things that will embarrass us both. Go home. We will speak tomorrow when '...*the morn, in russet mantle clad, Walks o'er the dew of yon high eastward hill...*'" He made a grand gesture and turned to go.

"Please don't send me away."

Jeremy threw up his arms. "Good grief! I am not sending you away. Quite the opposite. I am trying to save you from my demons."

"I am sure your demons are no worse than mine. Perhaps they should be introduced." Jeremy laughed sadly and walked on. Rory was quickly at his side. "Please sir, may I see your flat?"

"No."

"Just now, when you were talking about Miss Stewart, I saw someone I had never seen before, and I liked him."

"Ghosts, Rory. You saw a ghost."

"Then I shall make friends with your ghost."

Jeremy laughed sardonically. "What makes you think you can do that, when I never could?"

"Please sir, may I come?"

"No!"

"Why?"

"What makes you think you will like what you find?"

"Damn it, Jerry!" He grabbed Jeremy's arm and pulled him back. "Don't play this game tonight, it's too late. I'm tired of grovelling for every crumb."

"You called me 'Jerry'." He glared. "Brave boy."

"I know we're different in some ways."

"At least one." Jeremy pulled away.

"...but in most ways we're very much alike."

Jeremy paused a few feet from the entrance to his building, shook his head, and closed his eyes. "Yes. In most ways, we are very much alike."

"Then take me up to your bloody flat, fix me a bloody cup of coffee, and tell me about... Katie."

Jeremy stayed still. A lump formed in his throat. Roughly taking Rory's arm, he led him inside past the uniformed doorman, through the high arched entranceway.

Momentarily stunned by the size and grandeur of the lobby, Rory stood by, watching the concierge hand Jeremy his mail. "Would you like Miss Stewart's, as well, sir?"

"Um, no, thank you. She should be along presently. Good night, Vickers."

"Good night, sir." While keeping a professional demeanour, the concierge looked Rory up and down and smiled behind his eyes. Tired as he was, Rory blushed. He did not dare to look at Jeremy. The lift operator looked at Rory the same way. Without a word, he closed the gate, and the door, and took them to the fourth floor. There were four doors in the vestibule. Jeremy walked across to a door with the brass nameplate:

Mr. Jeremy O'Connell
Miss Katherine Stewart
(*Mr. and Mrs. Jeremy O'Connell*)

Jeremy unlocked the door and walked into the marble floored, mirrored foyer. To their left, a tall door opened onto a carpeted staircase. At the top of the stairs, another door stood open.

Jeremy's valet Max tottered in, rubbing his eyes like an off duty sentry. His uniform jacket was slightly crooked. "So sorry, sir. I was reading and dozed off." He hung their hats and coats in the closet.

Jeremy smiled. "Not to worry, Max. I told you not to wait up. This is Rory Cook."

Max looked delighted. "It is indeed. What a pleasure to meet you. I have enjoyed your performances, especially in The Scottish Play. You see, Mr. Cook, I always watch the dress rehearsals. Then I see the plays a month later. It is wonderful to see how the productions grow." He offered his hand.

Used to conventional servants, Rory enjoyed the informality, chuckled, and shook Max's hand. "Yes, that must be wonderful. Have you trod the boards yourself?"

"Lord no." Stifling a giggle, Max put a hand over his mouth. "I was a costumier. Toured with Mr. O'Connell some years ago."

Jeremy patted Max's shoulder. "I stole him away from the Scottish circuit."

"And very grateful I was too, sir." He started closing the door at the bottom of the staircase.

"Max," Jeremy whispered, lightly shaking his head.

"Very good sir?" Looking slightly puzzled, Max reopened the door. Rory watched their silent communication. "May I offer you gentlemen any refreshment?" He stood to attention.

Jeremy smiled. "I'll get whatever my young friend needs. You go on to bed."

"Thank you, sir. Good night, gentlemen." He made a small bow and left them alone.

Rory stared at the open door. "Max closed the door, because he thought I was..."

"Naturally," Jeremy chuckled. "Upstairs is Katie's flat. Evan has a room upstairs and another down here. When this bottom door is closed, he knows my flat is out-of-bounds." He paused, deciding how to proceed. "Katie's personal life should be no one's concern but her own, but, since you have her pegged so very wrongly, I will tell you the truth, this one time, and expect you never to broach the subject again. Agreed?"

Rory swallowed. "Agreed."

He gazed up the stairs. "You know that Katie came out of Variety, dancing in her family's act, *The Stewart Swans*. Their picture still hangs in the Red Lion. Simon Camden joined the act when he was eighteen and

Katie was thirteen. They became lovers when she was sixteen, and Simon left a year later.

"When Katie was twenty, she came to London to become an actress. That was when we met. She intended to live with Simon, but he took himself off on tour and has been on tour, off-and-on, for the past fifteen years. That first season, living alone, Katie was sending all her earnings to her family. Keeping nothing for herself, she was forced to sleep on her dressing-room floor.

"I had a small flat, so I took her in to live with me and, with the exception of my interim tour, we lived together, in that small flat, for five years. We had a fake marriage certificate and it all looked terribly respectable." Rory held up his hand and Jeremy chuckled wearily. "And to answer your next question: Yes! We slept in the same bed for five years and I never made love to the woman. Shall I go on?"

Rory swallowed hard. "Yes, sir. Please, go on."

"While I was away on tour, Eric Bates engaged Katie. Knowing Hilda Bates as well as you do, you can well imagine why he fell in love with Katie. Later, he hired me. Eventually Katie became pregnant. I offered to marry her. She thought it a bad idea, but agreed to let me play father. We moved into these flats just before Evan was born.

"Hilda was outraged of course, so Eric swore the child was mine and not his. I never denied it, but she never believed it. After that, Eric stuck close to Hilda's money, played the model husband, and left Katie alone. Simon Camden sails into town for a couple of weeks, most years. Occasionally, he stages a play in London. He stays with Katie, but spends some nights away. We never ask where."

Rory sprung to attention. "But... Well... if Mr. Camden sees other women... doesn't Miss Stewart mind?"

"Katie has tolerated Simon's affairs since she was a child. She has tolerated my affairs for fifteen years. She is the most tolerant woman in England and loves us both -- warts and all. So, except for Simon's visits, Katie has been living like a nun.

"Years ago, I encouraged her to go out. As you say, she has endless invitations. She found the men to be pompous or brutish and now refuses everyone. Last year, I cast Owen Freeman to play opposite her in *Duchess of Malfi*. It was a stroke of genius. On-stage, they are magic together. The chemistry was enough to continue off-stage and I encouraged their affair. Even though she really does not like him, he is fabulously handsome, apparently well endowed, and she is allowing him to pleasure her in a way she has not enjoyed, possibly ever."

By now, Rory's eyes were like cartwheels. "You mean, Owen is only Miss Stewart's third lover?"

"Wasn't I clear?"

"Do you two still..?"

"Constantly. I adore cuddling that luscious female. She is soft and sweet, and…"

"But you never..?"

Rolling his eyes again, Jeremy walked into the drawing room. "These windows have a clear view of the sunrise."

He pulled velvet drapes back from the wide windows, and the faint glow of several-hundred streetlights glimmered through the glass. He sat on a plush sofa, and Rory sat next to him. A flaming-pink streak blazed across the black horizon. On the street below, lamplights started going dark. Jeremy imagined hundreds of lamplighters lowering the gas on thousands of lamps, and knocking on all the windows they passed. Common people owned no clocks. If they missed that early knock and overslept, they could lose their jobs. The last streetlights went out as a pink blaze filled the sky.

Pretending to yawn, Jeremy stretched his arm along the back of the sofa, behind Rory's head. "I've been thinking about Evan." Rory looked startled and Jeremy smiled thoughtfully. "When he becomes a young man, in say nine or ten years, do you suppose that he and I will still be as close as we are now?"

"Of course you will."

Jeremy nodded. Keeping his gaze on the sunrise, he spoke gently. "Do you suppose there might be an occasion when he might need reassurance, and I might put a fatherly arm around his shoulder?"

"Certainly." Rory's face contorted, as if he were in pain.

Jeremy smiled kindly. "Then, would you mind very much if I put a fatherly arm around your shoulder right now?"

Rory swallowed. "I think I would like that very much."

*

Lester, Todd, and Elly walked the short blocks to Mrs. Potter's boardinghouse. Both young men were silly with drink and all three were giddy with fatigue. Arm-in-arm they sang,

" *'Oranges and lemons', say the bells of St. Clement's.*
'You owe me five farthings', say the bells of St. Martins.
'When will you pay me?' say the bells of Old Bailey.
'When I grow rich', say the bells of Shoreditch...."

A few feet from the entrance, Elly stopped. The men kept going and crashed into each other. Todd straightened up and tried to focus. "I say Miss Fielding, a bit of bad driving there." He tottered from side to side.

Lester started up the steps and she held him back. He blinked, trying to make both eyes look in the same direction. "This is the place, old girl, don't you recognize it? Bloody awful, but it is home."

She nervously bit her lip. "Will Meg and Peg be there?"

Todd shook his head. "Not bloody likely. The regular blokes in town get paid Friday night. They like to show a girl a good time and our two are always available. Come on, it's bloody cold." He started up the steps again.

Elly held him back. "I can't sleep in that room, that bed, the linen, it's putrid."

Lester laughed, "So's ours, right Toddy?" He lost his balance and sat down the step. "Potter's got some bed linen stashed in the cellar, doesn't she, Todd?"

"There's rats in that cellar, big buggers."

Lester saw the horror on Elly's face. "Don't worry Miss Fielding, the rats don't bother. Come on Toddy, let's see what we can find."

The front door was unlocked and they went inside. Elly held the door, letting in enough street light so Lester and Todd could strike a match and light candle stubs. They walked through the kitchen to the cellar door and the men disappeared into the dark. Elly heard a crash, a dull thud, and a lot of cursing. Finally, they resurfaced holding piles of bed linens.

Lester smiled like a Cheshire Cat. "We can talk, you know. Mrs. Lynn's deaf, Peter's a sport, Potter takes a sleeping powder, and I don't give a hoot about the old women." Elly took all three candles, Todd took the linen, Lester filled two coal buckets, and they all went upstairs.

When they reached the girls' room, Todd put the linens on the table and looked around. "Christ almighty, I thought our room was a pigsty."

Lester and Elly stripped the bed. Elly knew what to expect, but Lester was horrified. "This is disgusting!" They rolled the soiled linen into a ball, remade the bed, and took the clean leftovers downstairs.

Peter's door was open and Todd grinned. "Jolly good! Pete's with Mrs. Lynn, so I get his bed." He grabbed some clean linen and hurried inside.

The men's room was like the girls', only tidier. They also had one bed, and Elly tried to picture all three men inside it. "Where's Mr. Cook?"

Lester smirked, "Pretty shop girls also get paid on Friday. Lots of them fancy our Rory." Elly thought about this while she and Lester changed the bed, then went back up to the girls' room. Lester filled her stove and lit the coals. "There's not enough coal to last the night. Lucky the night's almost over." She smiled at his weak joke and he watched her in the bright glow. He touched her cheek and she jumped back.

"I'm sorry, Mr. Reid. You're very kind. Thanks so much for helping me." His moon-shaped face was bright in the firelight. His smile was inviting. His plump, comfortable body might have been nice to hug, but she would never let another man touch her, not ever.

"Well, good night then. Sweet dreams." He left her alone.

Chapter 6

Saturday, December 19, 1903

Thin shafts of bright winter sunlight streamed through crevices in Jeremy O'Connell's velvet drapes. He opened his eyes and blessed Max for silently preparing the cheery coal fire sizzling in the hearth. The clock next to the bed read 1:03. He allowed himself a long, sensual yawn, then walked to the window and pulled the curtain-rope. As the drapes separated, white sunlight flooded the room, making his magnificent bedroom look like a stage set from Molière. Gazing down onto the busy street, he remembered last night. The intensity of feelings flooded back. Rory and he were on that street, together. Rory was groveling, absolutely begging to be taken home. *Whatever possessed me? It was the first time we battled and he won. He had called me, "Jerry." We watched the sunrise.*

Remembering the next part, his heart raced. He leaned against the curtains. *He let me put my arm around him. Thank God I didn't ask for more, lord knows I wanted to. He is absolute perfection.* Shaking off lust and longing, Jeremy tossed on a dressing-gown, and went to check on Rory. The guest room door was ajar and a fire sizzled in that hearth. Rory was asleep, his wavy yellow hair spread like a halo over the pillow. Jerry smiled at the endearing picture. He tiptoed to the wardrobe, found a silk dressing-gown, laid it across the foot of the bed, and returned to his room.

An hour later, Rory finally surfaced. He looked dishevelled, but adorable, wrapped in a dressing-gown. Jeremy was bathed and shaved, wearing a tartan smoking jacket, sitting at the table, reading the paper. He looked up and smiled. "Good afternoon. I trust you slept well."

"Yes, thanks." He fingered the fine silk of the dressing-gown. "This is magnificent."

"It's Stephen's. He used to play violin in the pit orchestra. Now, he's joined a chamber orchestra, touring the continent. So what would you like first, breakfast or a bath?"

Rory touched his rough chin. "A bath, please, and a shave."

"As you wish. You will find everything you need. Max has gone to the shops, so we are quite alone. If you want a rubber duck, there's a variety in the cupboard."

Rory laughed, grateful to break the tension. "Thanks ever so much. I'll be fine without one."

"And please, help yourself to Stephen's clothes. I paid for most of them, and hate seeing them unused."

"That is more than kind. Thanks very much, indeed." Smiling gratefully, he turned to go, then paused. "Mr. O'Connell?" He stared at the floor.

"Hmm?" Jeremy waited with a half-smile on his lips.

"Tonight, when we're back at the theatre…"

Jeremy raised an eyebrow, chuckling, "I won't tell, if you won't tell."

Rory's cheeks flamed red. "There is nothing *to* tell, but the chaps…"

"They would never let you hear the end of it. I quite understand." He crossed his legs. "Oh, by the way, you needn't be concerned about Elly Fielding. She fancies you."

"She does?" He grinned, then frowned again. "But at supper last night, every time…"

"I saw her shy away from you. It was curious. She was comfortable with Lester because he was clowning, but I wonder what happened after they returned home. If he made any sort of romantic gesture, she probably reacted the same way to him." He put a finger over his lips. "I do not know the girl at all, but I fear she has been treated badly -- by men."

Rory sat down, concentrating. "What do you mean, 'treated badly'? You don't think that she has been, well… raped or something."

Jeremy shrugged. "I don't know. It is just a feeling. I hope that I am entirely wrong."

"Well, if she has been… whatever. What can I do?"

"Well now, that depends on what you want from her."

He leaned forward. "I want her to trust me."

"Why, so you can violate her?" Rory opened his mouth and Jeremy cut him off. "You must decide what you want, before you plunge into her life…" He raised an eyebrow, "…so to speak." Rory blushed again, and Jeremy smiled at his double-entendre. "She is beautiful, intelligent, and I want to make her into an actress. If her feelings are as bottled up as they seem to be, that may be a daunting assignment."

He smiled nonchalantly. "Please, for all our sakes, decide what you want from her, before you act. Do you wish to be her lover, her friend, her colleague, her brother, her husband, what?" He leaned in, pointing a finger. "Seriously, Rory. Elly is not Peg, so be careful. I do not want her running away just because a love affair sours. So which do you prefer, coffee or tea?"

Rory took a moment, then smiled. "Coffee, thanks,"

*

That evening, Elly Fielding planned to look at the stage set for *The Magistrate*, then go into the stalls and watch the play. When she reached stage level, she heard laughter and saw backstage workers outside Katherine Stewart's dressing room. She hid in the shadows, watching Katherine greet scene-shifters, costumers, and char women. Her honey blond hair was tied up in a stylish twist. Long sparkling earrings dangled against her cheeks and a matching necklace hugged her throat. A pale-blue silk dressing-gown wrapped gracefully, setting off her clear blue eyes. Her natural style stage makeup looked very beautiful, and very different from Lady Macbeth. She handed her dresser a brightly wrapped package. "Happy Birthday, Eileen. It's from all of us."

The older woman broke into a toothy grin and tore off the paper. Inside was a gilt framed photograph. "Oh, m' gracious!" Tears filled her eyes and she wiped them away with the palm of her hand. "The kids are growin' so fast. I been wantin' a photo fer ever so long. Oh, Miss Katherine." She threw herself in Katherine's arms, then hugged the others.

*

Katherine saw Elly, nearly a silhouette in the shadows. The girl's thin frame and long hair reminded her of herself at that age. *I was always cold and hungry. Is she?* "Hello, Miss Fielding." Smiling warmly, she took Elly's hand and pulled her into the light.

Elly smiled shyly. "Please call me Elly. You look so beautiful Miss Stewart, like a perfect china doll."

Katherine laughed. "How sweet. Please come in." She led Elly into her dressing room. It was the same size as Jeremy O'Connell's, but decorated much more simply. A basket of shining apples stood invitingly. Katherine saw the girl's hungry eyes. "Please help yourself. An admirer sent these, and we've got a whole bushel at home." She sat at her dressing table, looked into the mirror, and checked her makeup.

Elly devoured an apple, while studying framed photographs hanging on the wall. One was a young man in black, holding a skull. The inscription read,

To Darling Kathy,
My first and only love.
Simon Camden

Elly was thrilled. "Oh my, I saw Simon Camden play Hamlet when I was little. Every summer, touring companies stopped near our village." Her eyes were like saucers as she stared at another remarkable photograph. A slender young man, in a tight fitting white suit, gracefully lifted a beautiful woman high over his head. Her arms spread wide and they looked like a single graceful swan, ready for flight. "Is that Mr. Camden, as well?"

As she finished her lip rouge, Katherine watched Elly's reflection in the mirror. "That is Simon and me. I was sixteen. He was twenty-one. We were the Stewart Swans, headliners, in Variety."

"I didn't know you were a dancer."

"My entire life. I joined my family's act as soon as I could walk. Please, have another apple. Come back after the show and take the basket to the boardinghouse. Just make sure you keep some for yourself. Please sit down."

Elly tossed her apple core into a dust bin and perched on the edge of a chair. "You're so kind. Everyone will be very grateful."

"You obviously survived your first night at Mrs. Potter's."

Elly nodded sheepishly. "I was so afraid, but Miss O'Mally and Miss Lamoor weren't there. Mr. Reid found clean bed sheets in the cellar and we changed the beds. It was frightfully cold, but I found a heavy quilt in the attic and slept very well." Katherine smiled and Elly's courage grew. "That was a lovely birthday photograph, you gave the lady."

"Eileen's been my dresser for twelve years. She's like a mother to me. She supports a good-for-nothing husband and all those delightful children. I was so pleased we could do something special for her birthday. When's your birthday?" She powered her face.

Embarrassed, Elly looked down and whispered. "Next week."

"Really? What day?"

"The twenty-third."

"You were a Christmas baby. Your mother must have been thrilled."

"My mother died the night I was born."

"Oh my dear, I'm so sorry." She turned to face the girl.

Elly smiled self-consciously. "It's all right. I never knew her, so I never missed her."

"Are you an only child?"

"Yes."

"Did your father remarry?"

"No."

"Who brought you up?"

"My aunt. When I was fourteen, I was sent away to school. It was wonderful."

Katherine made a quick mental inventory. Something was odd. Elly obviously came from money, but the way she devoured that apple, she was starving. "Is your aunt pleased that you're becoming an actress?"

Elly paled. "My family has no money and I have no dowry. I can never marry and have to make my own way."

"There was money enough for your schooling."

"A family friend paid my tuition."

"But she won't provide a dowry? Apprentices earn no wages. If you need to make your own way, perhaps you should find work that pays a wage."

Elly looked frightened. "I've thought of that, but I don't want to do anything else. I want to be an actress. Miss O'Mally and Miss Lamoor find work."

Katherine rolled her eyes, then smiled reassuringly. "Not to worry. You're lovely. Jerry told me you have wonderful potential, and he's never wrong. If you're willing to study very hard, and go hungry..."

"I am. I promise. I'll do anything that's asked of me. I'm clever. I learn fast. You'll never hear me complain. Not ever!"

Katherine laughed warmly. "I believe you. With that kind of passion, you're sure to succeed. You begin acting classes next week. I hope Jerry will be kind."

*

That evening, Jeremy O'Connell sailed through *The Magistrate* in an especially good mood. The night before, Rory had forced him to review his long history with Katherine Stewart. He was pleasantly surprised by the very real affection he still felt for her. As always, the silly comedy had ended with the husband and wife kissing. Tonight, he kissed Katherine passionately. The final curtain fell and they were still in a tight clutch. When they pulled apart for the curtain-call, she was breathless, Jeremy was ecstatic, and her young lover Owen Freeman was seething. The moment the stage lights came on, Owen sped to Katherine's side, reclaiming stolen property.

Assuming Owen would stay with Katherine overnight; Jeremy wanted Evan in his downstairs flat, before they arrived. Men were arrested for wearing makeup on public streets, so Jeremy scurried home through dark shadows. He found the key for Katherine's flat and opened her door.

Evan heard the lock turn and ran to the foyer. He was in his night clothes, but very wide awake. "You're early, Daddy. How was the show?"

"Exceptional, dear boy, truly." He put his hand on Evan's head. "I am going to start staging *The Tempest*. Would you like to help me?"

"Oh, may I, please? Yes, yes!" He raced down the staircase to Jeremy's flat. Jeremy followed, closing the door at the top of the stairs.

A miniature stage set was on the dining room table. Evan pulled himself onto a chair and carefully moved tiny, exquisitely carved ivory figurines, costumed for the play. "Why won't Mummy be in the play?"

"Because she is stubborn as a mule. She insists that she is too old to play a girl of fifteen." Jeremy shrugged. "You and I both know that is absolute rubbish, but she is convinced, and that-is-that. If she thinks she is getting time off, she is very much mistaken. I need her eyes and ears, whether or not she is on the stage. Now, I must take off this paint." He walked to his bedroom and Evan followed.

"Can't I be in the play?"

"No."

"Why?"

"Because Shakespeare didn't want you in the play."

"He didn't want Miss Fielding in the play either, but she's got a part."

Jeremy hung up his suit jacket and threw his soiled shirt into a wicker basket. "Elly Fielding does not have a part. She is a super'. Miranda is the only woman in the play and she will be played by Sandra Lindford. Elly will practically be part of the scenery, a kind of symbol for all that is beautiful on the island: Miranda's innocence, Prospero's magic, all those things that must be left behind." He went into the bathroom and Evan followed.

"Why does Elly get to play it?"

"Because she is a beautiful young girl."

"I'm young."

"You are not a girl."

"Does it have to be a girl?"

"Yes."

"Why?"

"Because Prospero is a man, and men like beautiful girls."

"Not all men like girls." Evan spoke the simple truth, and Jeremy smiled.

"On stage, all men like girls."

Evan looked at the floor and shuffled his feet. "In Shakespeare's time, boys played girls. I could wear a wig. I still don't see why I can't play it."

Jeremy sighed, opened a tub of lard, and rubbed some into his face. "There - is - no - role." Evan looked totally dejected, and Jeremy shook his head. "Elly is going to spend most of the play sitting on a rock." Evan's expression grew even more miserable and Jeremy started laughing. "You are as stubborn as your mother. There will be another part for you, soon enough."

"When?"

"Perhaps in the next play."

"But the next play won't be until September. I can't wait that long."

Jeremy threw up his hands. "Can't wait that long?" He forced a frown and glared down. "How old are you?"

Evan threw up his hands, copying the gesture. "You know how old I am, I'm nine."

"And are you planning on…"

"...reaching ten?" Evan finished the phrase and stamped his foot. Jeremy burst out laughing, and Evan looked up with sorrowful blue eyes, exactly like his mother's. "You're sure you couldn't find even a small part for a small boy?"

Jeremy's reading was cold. "No - chance - at - all."

Evan heaved a final despair-filled sigh, yawned, and stretched. "Is Owen staying with Mummy?"

"I believe so."

Almost asleep, Evan allowed Jeremy to tuck him into bed, and turn off the light. Jeremy was almost out the door when he heard a sleepy, "I like Owen."

Jeremy chuckled. "So do I." He took two steps and...

"I like Uncle Eric better."

"So do I."

"I like Uncle Simon better than Uncle Eric."

"So do I, now go to sleep."

"I love you best of all."

Sighing happily, Jeremy walked back and sat on the edge of the bed. Evan reached his thin arms around Jeremy's neck and kissed his cheek. Jeremy kissed Evan's forehead, and pulled the covers around him.

"Mummy's never cross when she sleeps with you. Why don't you get married? We could take down those stupid doors between the floors. I could have all my things in one room..." Finally the boy was truly asleep. Jeremy pulled the door almost closed and went back to staging *The Tempest*.

It was very late when he finally went to bed. Staging a play on paper, and imagining his perfect production was pure joy. He dreaded the first rehearsals. The actors always brought their own ideas. After explaining his wants, they invariably misunderstood. He would become a monster, forcing them to do what he wanted. On opening night, if he did his job, his perfect vision would appear on the stage. The play would be a triumph.

He fell into a deep dreamless sleep, and only woke when the covers were pulled up. Katherine slid beside him. He opened one eye. "I thought you were with Adonis."

"I was. I couldn't stand it."

"Umm." He shut the eye and went back to sleep.

When Katherine woke, he was lying on his side, smiling.

She smiled back. "Good morning, darling."

"Good morning, my love." They exchanged a cordial kiss. She rolled over, snuggling her back against his front. He put his arms around her. "Umm, you feel good." They were silent for few minutes. He whispered, "What are you doing here?" His hot breath tickled her ear.

"Owen's an extraordinary lover, but he's such a bore. Whenever we try to have a conversation, we row. I couldn't stand another, so I ran away."

"You left that man upstairs, in your bed?"

She nodded, smiling guiltily.

"That's funny." Laughing loudly, he fell back onto his pillow.

"Speaking of beds, last night I saw Rory Cook wearing Stephen's brown suit."

Embarrassed, Jeremy closed his eyes. "Indeed. Rory followed me home. I gave him Stephen's bed, breakfast, a suit, and nothing more."

She faced him. Her eyes were full of concern. "You're in love with him, aren't you?"

He shrugged. "I suppose. Speaking of love… You wouldn't want to marry me, would you? Forsaking all others and all that?" He kissed her nose.

She lay back with a half-smile. "The man I'm in love with tells me he's in love with someone else, then proposes marriage practically in the same breath. I'll have to think about that one." His cheeks flushed and Katherine chuckled, "I do wish there was something more I could do for you."

"How absurd! Whatever more could you do, except perhaps turn yourself into a boy."

"That's very intriguing. Would you like me to be a boy?"

"No, just teasing." He laughed, kissing her ear.

"That tickles." She pulled away, giggling. "At times I have wished that I could be a boy, for you."

"What a silly girl you are." He rolled his eyes in exaggerated disdain. "You're sugar…" He gently squeezed her nipple. "…and spice," He tickled his fingers over her firm belly, "…and everything…" His hand moved down between her legs, "…nice." She closed her eyes as his hand searched under the covers, pulling up her nightdress. Finding her soft opening, he probed with gentle fingers and nuzzled his mouth over her

63

ear. "Umm, you're all warm and juicy. I'm pleased I still have that effect on you."

She gasped, "You've had that effect on me since the first moment I laid eyes on you, fifteen-years-ago." Turning her face, her mouth found his. They kissed passionately as his fingers rubbed. Her soft flesh hardened into a round marble and he was thrilled, knowing he was thrilling her.

Suddenly, her body tensed, her legs pulled hard together, and her heart raced. She clung to him, breathing hard. When he smiled smugly, she laughed. "Naughty boy. You're all snails and nails and puppy dogs' tails." Touching his face, she ran one finger over his forehead, along his eyebrow, cheek bone, down his nose and along his lips. He kissed it in passing. Her hand slid down his neck, and over his chest.

When it passed his ribs he said, "Don't even think it."

"Why not? It's been a long time."

"Yes, it has."

"I've had mine."

He laughed. "Yes, you have… in excess."

"You need it."

He thought for a moment. "Yes, I do." He lay on his back, stretched his arms, and put his hands behind his head. Her hand continued down until it rested between his legs. He smiled and let out a contented sigh. Very gently, using both hands, she began to stroke his very eager cock. He stretched and groaned with pleasure. "Ah, Katie, you always did have magnificent hands." She continued to pull, lift, gently squeeze, and finally rub until his body twisted, then collapsed back, totally relaxed. The worry lines left his face. She cuddled against him, and fell asleep.

Chapter 7

Sunday, December 20, 1903

The stage-doorkeeper handed Elly two notes. " 'ello, Miss Fielding. You'll 'ave to sign in, from now on." He pointed to a blackboard on the wall. A piece of chalk hung on a string.

Happy adrenaline rushed as she took the chalk and read down the list: *Arthur Anderson, Eric Bates, Michael Burns, Nancy Cushman, Elly Fielding* ... She carefully initialed, E.F., next to her name. *Jeremy O'Connell* was in the middle. *Katherine Stewart* was at the end. "Thanks, Mr. Adams." She smiled, opened her mail, and hurried to the lady's washroom.

Miss Fielding,
Mr. Bates said I was to give you a schedule. Monday we're dark. Tuesday at
10:00 report to Veronica Wallace, costume designer or Connie Vickers, costume-mistress, in the costume shop. At 12:00, go up the peacock's nest, to Eugene the wig-master. Acting class will be in the rehearsal hall at 1:00.
Cheers,
Eddy Edwards

Elly caught her breath. Surely she would not be expected to do anything in an acting class? She read the second note.

Elly,
I hope you're all right. The Actress and Villain is closed on Sundays, so we all eat at the Red Lion after the matinee. Something important has come up, so let me buy you a meal, and we'll talk.
Michael

She took a quick wash and went into the crowded stalls for the *Macbeth* matinee. Old Jim greeted her. " 'ello, love. Y' better keep out o' sight today. Hilda Bates and 'er family are in the box. She don't like to see actors in the 'ouse. Says they're riffraff." Elly saw Hilda Bates, her elderly parents, and two plain daughters. They sat as silently as visitors at a wake. Old Jim pulled Elly from sight as the houselights dimmed.

As soon as the final curtain fell, Elly hurried across the street to the Red Lion Pub. It was grander than *The Actress and Villain* and nearly empty. Her leather heels clipped along the dark-wood floor. She paused in front of an old photo in a worn frame. Six dancers, dressed like white birds, posed next to a large placard: *The Stewart Swans*. A huge carved mirror hung next to the bar. She saw her reflection, and tried to smooth her impossibly wrinkled skirt. Her hair was in a neat braid down her back.

A door near the bar opened and wonderful smells poured from the kitchen. A slender man with a huge gray beard appeared. He squinted, smiled, and pointed a bent finger. "Tall - thin - red 'air - green eyes - pretty as a picture - You must be the new apprentice. I'm Jamie Jamison, owner of this establishment." He held up his disfigured hand. "An' this 'ere's why I left show business. I were a Pyro-Magician. Fire eatin', fire throwin', flames explodin' all over the place." He pointed to the photo of the Stewart Swans. "Knew Kathy Stewart since she were a baby."

Suddenly, the pub was alive with theatre patrons. Elly smiled at Jamie, but anxiously watched the door. When the actors started coming in, she hurried past Rory and Lester, to Michael. "I got your note. What is it you…?"

He squeezed her arm and walked up to the bar. "Hello Jamie, can I please have a pint, a lemonade, and two of your specials." Michael took the drinks.

Elly followed him to a corner booth and sat facing him. "You're so kind. Someday I hope I can repay your generosity."

"Don't worry about it. I was an apprentice. People fed me." He nervously drummed his fingers on the table, then took a long drink. "Well, you've survived two nights, freezing and starving at Potter's. If you stay, you can count on freezing and starving for at least a year. The other apprentices manage to scrounge a living, but…"

"I will too."

"How?" He looked her in the eye. "The boys build sets for slave wages. Meg and Peg… " He shook his head.

She leaned forward, whispering, "You told me, they're tarts. I don't know what I'll do, but I'll find some sort of work. I'm clever, you'll see. I'll be fine."

A server brought their food and they ate silently. When Michael's plate was clean, he reached into his jacket pocket and pulled out two envelopes. "Yesterday, I got these from Rob. The first one was so formal, I didn't know why he'd written it. The late post brought the second letter, and it all became clear." He handed her the two letters.

Elly opened the first one.

My Dear Michael,

I trust you are well. Things are looking very good for my exhibition. The paintings have arrived safely, and you can imagine how I look forward to seeing them displayed. Unfortunately, I can only stay two nights in London. My mother is visiting with her sister and I need to call on them before the start of term.

I am so looking forward to Macbeth. *See you in a fortnight.*

Your Friend,

Robert Dennison

Elly handed the letter back, and opened the second.

Mike -

I know I would have heard from you if Elisa wasn't safe and well. Bless you for helping her.

I was insane to think that she could just disappear. When she was found missing, her teacher telegraphed her father. The return telegram said she was not at home, but may have run away to her mother's family in Germany. Her father is arriving here, tomorrow. He has threatened to call in Scotland Yard, or a private investigator. I could go to prison.

They are watching the post, so I bribed the milkman to mail this letter from
another village. If you write back, you must not mention her by name. Instead, say that the Christmas box arrived safely or, God forbid was damaged, or misplaced. I am going mad.

I was an ass not to have anticipated this. If Elisa's clothes are not discovered with my paintings, she should be safe. If she is in London when I arrive, I may be watched, and she may be in danger. I will leave as soon as I can.

I feel like a shit, getting you involved. It all seemed simple and sensible at the time. I adore Elisa, but wonder if I have done her a disservice. I wish I had left the matter alone.

Please tell her what has happened, or let her read this letter. I have never felt so wretched.

Rob

Elly read the letter over three times before handing it back.

Michael tucked both letters into his jacket pocket. "After reading the second one, I hoped you had changed your mind about all this, and decided to go home."

"Go home!" Her heart pounded. "I can never go home."

"Why? Wait, I almost forgot." Reaching into another pocket, he pulled out a small square of heavy art paper. "This was inside the second letter." She took the curious package. All four corners had been folded into the center and sealed together with blue sealing wax. On the front of the art paper, a lovely pink and blue rose was sketched around the name, ELLY. She broke the seal. Robert's flowers and vines delicately bordered his beautifully penned words.

My Dearest Darling Elly,

My single wish in life is that I could turn back the clock and play again that last evening. Things should have been very different. You can never know how much I care for you, and how desperately I want you near me. All those months of watching you, wanting you, not being able to touch you, and then, when we were finally together, misunderstanding you so completely. I shall never forgive myself. Would to God we could be together now, so I could try to make amends. You are the dearest thing in my life.

By now, you will have read my letter to Michael. Rest assured that I will do you no further damage. I must be in London for the gallery opening and Michael's play. In the event that I am being watched, I will return home immediately after and remove any possible danger to you.

Please try to forgive me. I love you.
Robert

Tears welled in her eyes. She folded the art paper and put it into her purse.

Michael stared at his empty plate. "This is out of my league. I don't know what to do. When I ran away to become an actor, no one cared enough to fetch me home."

"Do we have to do anything? No one knows I'm here. If I collect my boxes before he arrives, I'll be safe. Robert said so." She smiled hopefully. "I don't want to cause any trouble. I never thought this..."

His eyes bulged. "It's very plain that no one thought at all, especially me. You're under-age and I may be in a lot of trouble."

"But, that's not possible. *You've* done nothing wrong."

Michael drummed his fingers on the table. "The only people who know your real name are Bates, O'Connell, and Eddy."

"You can't tell them I've run away." Her breathing was fast and irregular.

"I have to tell them. They're harbouring an underage fugitive." He stood up and looked around the crowded pub. Eric Bates was eating with his family. Jeremy O'Connell and Katherine Stewart were finishing their meal. Eddy was drinking with some of the crew. "The snug is almost never used." He gestured to a small private dining room. "Go and wait in there." He started toward Eric Bates.

*

Jeremy O'Connell had just finished eating when Michael Burns begged five minutes of his time, in the snug. Eddy Edwards joined them, smiling cordially. Eric Bates raced after them, cursing, "Bloody hell, Burns! My whole family is here. What the devil's so important you had to interrupt my dinner?" He raced ahead into the snug, and glowered at Elly Fielding standing stiffly, staring at the floor. "What's she doing here?"

Michael looked at Elly and shut the door. "I'm sorry to disturb your afternoon, gentlemen, but you're the only people in London who know Miss Fielding's real name. Her family has decided they want her back and may go to extreme measures to find her."

"Find her?" Eric glared at Elly. "You're a bloody runaway?" She nodded. "How old are you?"

69

She spoke calmly. "Eighteen sir. In three days."

"Seventeen!" He bellowed and she shuddered. "The girl is bloody seventeen. Pack her up, and send her home." He stormed toward the door, but Elly raced in front of him, blocking his way.

She stared him straight in the eye. "Please, sir. I cannot go home." Her hands were tight fists, squeezing the fabric on her skirt. Labored breaths pulsed her thin ribcage, but her pale face showed no emotion. Tears welled in her huge green eyes but miraculously stayed where they were. The effect was startling.

Eric took a moment, then shouted at Eddy, "Get her on the next train out of here." Jeremy grabbed his arm. "Eric, let me find out what this is all about. Go back to your family."

He scowled. "A scandal could close us down."

Jeremy pulled him into a corner, whispering, "Eric, look at the girl. She is fabulously beautiful. She could make us a fortune."

"She could also cost us a fortune."

"I am aware of that and I will not do anything stupid."

Eric sighed. "See that you don't. I want a proper solution, or the girl's gone... Tonight!" He turned to leave as Rory Cook burst through the door, nearly knocking him down.

"Sorry, Gov'."

Rory cowered as Eric yelled, "Get out of here, Cook. This is no business of yours."

Rory saw Elly standing alone facing four angry men. Wanting to protect her, but having no idea what was happening, he stood his ground. Jeremy gently moved Eric toward the door. "I - will - deal - with - this. Go back to your family."

Eric glowered and left.

Jeremy closed the door and leaned against it. Rory moved toward Elly, but she stiffened, as if warning him to keep his distance. Jeremy was thrilled. She was magnificent. If he could teach her to harness that passion, she would... a vein pulsed in her temple. "Sit down, Miss Fielding." He put a hand on her shoulder and gently pushed her into a chair. Her composure broke slightly. A soft sniffle wrinkled her nose and the vein in her forehead flattened.

Eddy put his hands behind his back. An unruly forelock fell over his eyes, as he rocked on his flat feet and forced a smile. "If anyone asks me,

I never heard of... Umm... what was that lady's name?" He smiled at Elly and looked to Jeremy. "Can I go now, sir?"

Jeremy nodded and Eddy slipped out. Jeremy kept the door open for Rory. "Mr. Cook, This is no concern of yours."

Rory stared at Elly, looking pale and ill. "Perhaps not, sir. But I would like it to be."

Michael threw up his hands. "Oh, this is brilliant. One bloke's already ruined his life for her, and here's another waiting in the queue."

Elly was horrified. "That's not true."

Jeremy slammed the door. "Very well! Mr. Burns and Mr. Cook, by design or misadventure we all seem to be involved in Miss Fielding's welfare. Therefore, I suggest we proceed with the utmost speed, order, and logic." He pulled up a chair, sat down and commanded. "Please - sit - down!" They obeyed. "Mr. Burns, be so kind as to tell me all you know of this affair."

Michael sighed deeply and recounted his long friendship with painter Robert Dennison. "Yesterday, two letters arrived." Jeremy raised an eyebrow and held out his hand. Michael gave him the letters and nodded toward Elly. "There was a note inside the second letter. It was addressed to her. I haven't read it."

Jeremy read the first letter then passed it to Rory. As he read the second letter, his eyes narrowed. He handed that letter to Rory, and looked at Elly. "There is no mention of your mother."

"She's dead, sir."

"Her family is in Germany?"

"Yes sir, but I don't know them."

"You never met?"

"Once, when I was little. They wanted to take me to live with them in Germany. I wanted to go."

"Why?"

"I was not happy at home."

"Why?" She tensed, so he did not press her. Instead, he turned to Rory. "Mr. Cook."

"Sir."

"You were for a time a student of the law."

"Yes, sir."

71

"In your studies, did you ever come across a circumstance similar to this?"

"Yes, sir. I wrote a paper on the 1861 Offense Against Young Persons Act."

"Do you believe that Mr. Burns is in danger from criminal prosecution?"

Rory thought for a moment then shook his head. "No, I do not."

Jeremy turned to Michael. "I know nothing of the law, but it appears to me that your role in this has been negligible. I cannot believe the same for your unfortunate friend, what's his name, Dennison? I don't know how I am going to deal with Miss Fielding, but I see no need for you to remain with us. May I keep these letters?"

"Please." He stood, eager to go. "We're off tomorrow. How will I know what you've decided?"

"If there is anything you need to know, I shall send 'round to your flat. If you hear nothing, fear nothing."

"Thank you, sir." He sighed with relief. "You didn't need to get involved. I don't know why you did... but thank you." He offered his hand and Jeremy shook it firmly. Michael looked at Elly. "Whatever happens, Elisa, good luck. You're lovely. I hope you find whatever it is you're looking for. I'm terribly sorry about all this." He kissed her cheek and hurried out, closing the door behind him.

Elly turned to Jeremy. "Please sir. No one knows I'm here. There is no need to send me away. You've even changed my name."

Still as chiseled granite, Jeremy gathered his thoughts. When he looked up, Elly was white as a sheet. "Miss Fielding, whatever I decide to do may impact everyone at His Majesty's Theatre. It will most certainly impact *your* future, so I recommend that you think very carefully before answering my questions." She sat up, bravely meeting his gaze. "Why did you run away?"

She paused before speaking. "When I was a little girl, my father betrothed me to a man much older than himself."

Rory choked. Jeremy gave him a warning glare and turned back to Elly. "Who is this man?"

"Sir John Garingham. A landowner. He mines coal."

"A man of means is not a bad match."

Eyes wide, looking ready to leap up and scream, she clutched her hands in her lap, and forced herself to sit still. Her words clipped through clenched teeth. "It is not necessarily a good match, sir."

"Do you find the gentleman objectionable?"

Again, she measured her words. "The gentleman feels no fondness toward me, whatsoever. We share no interests and he finds no pleasure in anything that I do. When he visits, I am instructed to stay in my room. During meals, I am forbidden to speak, unless spoken to. When they have guests, I am expected to sing and play the piano, but Sir John talks throughout or leaves the room. When he does choose to see me in private, it is only to force his attentions." Her voice rose and her body tensed. "Since I was fourteen, I have had many bruises from fighting his unwelcome advances."

Rory stared at Jeremy, but clamped his mouth shut.

Jeremy showed no emotion. "Did your mother know of this betrothal?"

"She died the night I was born. Father told me I was conceived from sin and my mother died as punishment."

Jeremy blinked hard. "It is not uncommon for a young girl to be betrothed to an older man of financial means. The fact that you do not like him has no sway in this argument."

"But that is the *entire* argument."

"Then it is a very poor one. Childish fears do not warrant respect. You have given me no reason to keep you here and risk a scandal."

"There is one other thing. Robert Dennison believes that there must be an estate from my mother's family in Germany. My father has no money and Sir John has supported us my entire life. I have always been told that I must marry him, because I have no dowry. But Robert Dennison believes that Sir John would not have waited so long and spent so much money on my education, if I had nothing to bring to a marriage."

Jeremy wearily shook his head. "The state of your personal finances is irrelevant to His Majesty's Theatre. I am sorry, Miss Fielding." He stood and started for the door.

She lurched after him. "What if His Majesty's Theatre prevented a grave miscarriage of justice?"

"A what?" He glared at her.

"Surely the tabloids would enjoy such a story." She posed like a paperboy, frantically waving a scandal sheet. "Special Edition! Young Actress Saved By His Majesty's Theatre!"

Jeremy was stone-faced. "How about: Special Edition! His Majesty's Theatre Harbouring Young Fugitive!" He paused, reconsidering. "That is not bad, actually. Unless we knowingly broke the law. Since *you* told us that your name was Elly Fielding, we had no reason to suspect otherwise."

Elly and Rory exchanged hopeful glances.

Jeremy continued, thinking out loud. "I was involved in a very nasty scandal, some years back. The theatre did well by it, made money hand-over-fist. It did not hurt my career either, in the long run. The short run was bloody unpleasant."

He looked at Elly standing like Joan of Arc, young, tall, lean, eyes shining, poised for battle. She was an extraordinary girl. Perhaps she really could make them a fortune. He turned to Rory. "Mr. Cook. Just for the sake of argument, have you any legal knowledge of estate inheritance?"

"Yes sir." He leapt to his feet. His voice crackled with excitement. "There are many statutes regarding Law Of Real Property, Unfair Enrichment, and again, in the 1861 Offense Against Young Persons Act, there are clear provisions for defending properties of under-aged persons."

Elly pleaded, "There must be a law regarding the *neglect* of a young person whose estate is in danger of theft."

Rory stifled his excitement. "Of course there is. There are also laws regarding the wilful neglect of any persons who may be in imminent danger." He stared at Jeremy. "Should we knowingly abandon a person in peril..."

"She is not in peril." Jeremy threw up his hands.

Elly begged, "Please sir. If we can make my father believe that I actually have gone to Germany, then he will never find me. I have a new name. No one in London knows me."

Rory shook his head. "He can still find you, eventually, but at least he'd be delayed enough to... it would give us time to discover..." He fought to find the right words. "Miss Fielding, your father said that you were conceived from sin?" She nodded, humiliated by the memory. Rory's blue eyes shone with excitement. "What did he mean?"

She shook her head. "I never really thought…"

Jeremy messaged his temples. "Now, what are you on about?"

"You'll see in a moment, sir." His face was shining and eager. "Elly, is it possible that the man you regard as your father may indeed not be your father?"

"No. Of course he is my father." Her eyes were wide and her breathing erratic.

Rory pleaded, "Elly, please, this may be your salvation."

"'Salvation'? Do you call being illegitimate, 'salvation'?"

"Please, just try to think. What could your father have meant by those words?"

"I don't know. I don't want to know."

Jeremy nodded slowly. "This is good. The tabloids will devour it. How can one discover such things?"

"It is not difficult, if one can access the General Register of birth records. At any event, we need to buy time."

Elly concentrated, biting her lower lip. "If I knew my Aunt Elisa's address in Germany, I could write her a letter." She paced, thinking. "She would write back… then… No. That's no good. Father needs to think that *I* am in Germany." She stopped short. "I need to write my father a letter, have that letter taken to Germany, and posted back to England."

Rory continued her thought. "It doesn't need to be Germany. Anywhere out of the country will do."

Jeremy raised an eyebrow. "And how do you propose to accomplish that?"

Rory shrugged. "You know half of London, sir. Some acquaintance of yours must regularly cross the channel."

"I don't know half of London, actually, but Katie does." Jeremy took a moment, sighed wearily, and shook his head. "Go and ask her to come here." Rory sped toward the door. "…in ten minutes. I need ten minutes alone with Miss Fielding."

Rory stopped dead. He and Elly exchanged worried glances. "Of course, sir. I'll ask Miss Stewart to come… in ten minutes. Shall I explain the matter, or would you rather…?"

"I would rather."

"Yes sir." Rory gave Elly a reassuring smile and left.

When the door was closed, Jeremy put out my hand. "Show me the note."

Elly gasped. "I'm sorry sir, but it is of a very personal nature."

"At this moment, Miss - Elisa - Roundtree, you do not have the right to any personal…"

Before he could finish she handed it to him. He studied the heavy art paper. "He calls you 'Elly'?"

She nodded stiffly. "Yes, sir. You and he are the only ones who ever have."

Jeremy found that strangely amusing. He unfolded the paper and admired the magnificent artwork. As he read the words, sadness came over him. His guess had been correct. The poor girl had been abused by her father, her betrothed, and her school-master. Of course she was afraid of men. When he gave her back the note, she folded it very gently, and carefully tucked it into her purse. That tender treatment proved she was still in love.

Jeremy spoke quietly. "It seems that you and Robert Dennison have a history. How long have you known each other?"

"Forever, sir. Four months."

He tried not to laugh. "I suppose four months seems like forever when you are seventeen. What are your feelings for him?"

She hesitated. "I honestly don't know, sir. I thought I loved him… then I hated him… now, this very sweet note…"

"It is, indeed, a very sweet note. How long ago was this, 'last evening' he mentioned?"

She shuddered with humiliation. "The night before my audition. Last Thursday."

"Just four days ago?"

"Yes, sir."

"Good God!" He leapt from his chair. She could be pregnant. He should have listened to Eric and sent her home. Calming himself, breathing deeply, he remembered her beauty, and why he was going to all this trouble. She stared up with startling green eyes. Men would throw themselves at her feet. If she was not pregnant yet, she could be tomorrow. Why were women so stupid? How did they learn to protect themselves? From their mothers? This girl had no mother. Most women

knew nothing. Even Katie got caught. Perhaps she could talk to Elly…
No, he wouldn't ask her… Yes, he would. She would love it.

The door opened and Katherine edged her face through the crack. She
had a mischievous glint in her eye. "I seemed to have missed all the fun.
First Eric thunders out of here in a rage, then Eddy sneaks out. Michael
runs away as if escaping torture, and now Rory tells me about these
remarkable letters." She walked in and Rory followed, red in the face.

"I'm sorry sir. I told her that you wanted to explain everything, but
she…"

Jeremy glared at him, and Katherine chuckled. "It's my fault, Jerry. I
wheedled it out of him." Elly stared up with hopeful eyes. Katherine sent
her a reassuring wink, then looked back at Jeremy. "So, we need to get a
letter posted from Europe."

Jeremy posed, leaning back on a table, crossing his arms and legs.
"Yes, Missy-Know-All, we do."

She laughed then thought for a moment. "The only one I can think of
quickly is Ned Hereford. I had lunch with Isabelle this week. She told me
he's in Paris."

Jeremy put his hands over his face. "God save me from modern
witches. Oh yes, I am sure the good Lady Richfield will be delighted to
be involved."

Katherine ignored his clowning. "She'll love it. The season's only half
over and she's already bored silly."

Jeremy snorted. "You know I cannot abide that woman."

"You adore Isabelle. She is one of the few women who doesn't
genuflect when you pass."

"And what about her good brother? Will Ned play along with our
masquerade?"

"He loves actors and a good romance. He personally financed your
production of *Cupid's Messenger*, remember?"

"That was hardly the same thing."

"Well, I can't imagine him finding fault, and I can't think of anyone
else at short notice. Everyone is back home for Christmas."

"Where the devil is Simon Camden?"

"New York, I think." She glanced out a window. "It's starting to rain.
Let's continue this at the flat. I'll send one of the boys with a note and
ask Isabelle to come as quickly as she can. Agreed?"

Jeremy sighed heavily. "Oh, very well." He fluttered a hand. "Entreat the good Lady's assistance."

Rory stood up. "I'll take the note, if that's all right."

Jeremy rolled his eyes. "*Gallop apace, you fiery-footed steeds.*"

Elly cringed as Katherine wrote a few words on a calling card and handed it to Rory. "Here's the address. If she's at home, try to persuade her to come. If not, leave the card and come back to us."

Jeremy handed Rory the two letters. "If you can, explain the situation and ask her to read these."

"Yes sir. I'll be back as soon as I can." He started for the door.

"Wait!" Jeremy handed him some money. "Take a cab." Grateful, but slightly embarrassed, Rory thanked him and was gone. Jeremy started from the snug, then turned back. "Miss Fielding, while I get the coats, be so kind as to show Miss Stewart the note." Her eyes widened and she looked mortified. Jeremy sent Katherine a look that this was important, and left the women alone.

Chapter 8

Katherine, Elly, Evan, and Jeremy ran from a cab, through freezing drizzle, into their building's grand foyer. When they reached Katherine's fifth floor flat, all four were shivering and eager to get inside. A welcoming fire raged in the hearth. Katherine invited Elly into the drawing room. "Come in, dear. Warm yourself."

"Thank you, Miss Stewart. Your flat is beautiful." She breathed in the cheery glow of soft gaslights and the crackling fire. A dark-blue velvet sofa with matching easy chairs sat facing the fireplace. The walls were Wedgwood-blue and the ceiling a creamy-white. A large portrait of four-year-old Evan hung on one wall, and across the room, a landscape of the Scottish highlands. Christmas garlands dangled gaily over a polished brass chandelier, matching brass wall sconces, doorways, and hearth. A small fir tree, decorated with candles and shiny paper ornaments, stood in the corner.

Katherine's maid came from the kitchen. "Will y' be wantin' anything, Miss Stewart?"

"Yes please, Clara. We ate at the pub, but I'm hoping Lady Richfield will be coming."

Clara smiled. "She always likes m' cucumber sandwiches. Says I slice 'em thinnest in London, and I've got nice baby tarts. Promised Master Evan if 'e did well on 'is Latin…" Smiling happily, she trotted back to the kitchen.

Jeremy scowled, took Katherine's hand, pulled her into her bedroom, and shut the door. "You read the note?"

Yawning wearily, she sat down on the bed. "My goodness, this was a hard week, and yes, I read the note."

"What are we going to do?"

"About what?"

"The girl may be with child and probably doesn't even know it."

She yawned. "Oh, that." Exhausted, her eyes closed.

"Yes that!"

She forced her eyes to open. "Well, what can one do until one knows? We won't for a month."

He glared at her. "I bloody well know how it works, but I doubt that she does."

Katherine met his glare. "Since you're the bloody great teacher, go and teach her."

"What is the matter with you women? Can't you teach your daughters anything?"

She laughed at the incongruity. "Don't look at me, she's not mine to educate."

"Who, then? I don't see any other women volunteering."

"Mother of God! I'm a great example for a young girl." She closed her eyes.

"You are."

She waved her hands, as if to erase his words.

"You're a veritable vestal virgin compared to Isabelle. She's a pillar of society who's lured half the men in London into her bed."

"She's only typical of her class. Actually, she is not typical. Her children were all fathered by her husband."

The doorbell chimed. Jeremy's eyes bulged in exasperation as his hand flew to his chest. "Oh! Be still my heart."

Katherine glared. "Behave yourself. She's doing us a favor, if she's come at all." She forced herself from the comfort of her bed, took hold of his belt buckle, and pulled him from the room. "Do come along."

In a flurry of fur, feathers, and silk, Isabelle, Lady Richfield, cascaded through the foyer. "Kathy you angel, how marvelous of you to invite me into your adventure." She hugged Katherine, and presented Jeremy with the back of her hand. "Jerry, darling. How charming to see you."

He looked into her strikingly beautiful face, clicked his heels, bowed from the waist, and held her hand to his lips. She gurgled with delight. "Oh Kathy, how lucky you are to have such a man for your companion. I almost said, 'consort,' what a silly I am." She giggled and he glared at her insolence.

Katherine shot him a warning glance, as Rory sneaked into the room and stood against the wall. Evan ran into Isabelle's arms. She leaned down, squeezing him affectionately. "I left in such a flurry, I haven't a single treat for you tonight. And this must be Miss Fielding."

Elly lowered her eyes, took Isabelle's gloved hand, and curtsied. "How-do-you-do, Lady Richfield. You are very kind to have come."

Isabelle's eyebrow arched slightly, and Jeremy knew she was impressed by Elly's manners. "Not at all." Still holding Elly's hand, Isabelle studied the girl's pale face. "You look familiar. Have we met?"

Elly smiled shyly. "You are very kind to think so, Lady Richfield, but I only arrived in London three days ago. Before that, I was never out of Yorkshire."

"Ah, well, the last time I was in Yorkshire was... I've no idea." Smiling cordially, she let go of Elly's hand. "You have quite a champion in Mr. Cook," she looked around, "wherever he is." Rory hurried into her sightline and stared. Isabelle's bright cheeks and sensuous lips were framed by glossy chestnut hair. A beautifully styled dark turquoise frock showed off her full breasts, tiny waist, and shapely swaying hips. Her electric-blue eyes flashed and Rory blushed.

Jerry smiled to himself. Whatever Rory felt for Elly, just now, he only had eyes for Isabelle.

Katherine gestured to the dining room. "Isabelle, will you take tea?"

"Yes, thank you."

They moved to the dining room table, and Rory held Isabelle's chair. She smiled serenely, brushed against him, and took her seat. He looked weak-in-the-knees.

Katherine poured the tea, while Clara passed trays of food.

Evan's mouth quickly smeared with raspberry jam. "My cough is all better, Auntie Isabelle. The medicine you gave me tasted like these tarts. It was very good."

She nodded, "Capital! We can't have an actor with a bad throat, now can we?"

Jeremy helped himself to one of Evan's tarts. "Isabelle, you are brilliant with herbs. I don't know how you create everything from antiseptics to hair-tonic."

Isabelle chuckled, set down her teacup, and stared at Elly. "Oh, my!" Everyone was shocked into silence. "Jerry, you remember the painting you copied last summer, at the castle?"

"The Scott Lauder?"

Evan chirped, "Daddy put it behind the wardrobe, with his other paintings. You told me it's a picture of your mother and her twin sister, when they were young."

Jeremy followed Isabelle's gaze toward Elly. "There is a resemblance. Is that why she looks familiar to you?"

"I looked at that painting every day, growing up. She could have posed for it. Miss Fielding, I read the letters from your art-master. He referred to you by a different name."

"'Elisa,' ma'am. My mother was German. She named me after her sister. My mother's name was Bertha, but I don't know her maiden name. I know nothing of my German family."

"How much do you know about your English family?"

"I only have my father, ma'am, and his unmarried sister, my Aunt Lillian. They had an elder brother Charles, but he died before I was born. There is no one else."

"I wonder." She stayed looking at Elly. "Evan dear, could you fetch that painting?"

"Of course." He hurried downstairs to Jeremy's flat.

Smiling kindly, Isabelle tilted her head. "So, Miss Fielding, have you written your letter?"

"Not yet."

"Then, since you are not eating, please go and do it."

Jeremy thought for a moment. "Katie, do you have any plain writing paper?"

She shook her head. "All of mine is monogrammed, but Evan has some that's plain."

He stood up. "Right. I know where it is. Miss Fielding, follow me, please." He led Elly into Evan's room, found the stationery, pen, and ink. He pulled out the child-sized chair at the low school table and she sat down. He sat in the tutor's chair.

She thought for a moment, then began to write.

Dear Father,

When this letter reaches you, I shall be far away. I am not going to Uncle Otto and Aunt Elisa, because you could find me there and I do not wish to be found. Please give my love to Aunt Lillian and the servants. Tell them that I am well and that I miss them.

Jeremy nodded. "Your father needs to know what you are living on."

She shrugged sadly. "The same as I am living on here: charity."

A smile flashed across his face. "Score one for you. Although he may not believe it, you can add that no one at school aided your escape."

"Oh, right! Poor Robert." She bit her lip, then added,

They must be very cross with me at school, after all the extra lessons to catch me up. I can never finish now. It was hard keeping such an important secret from everyone, but I did it, and now I am safely away.

  Your Daughter,

Elisa Roundtree

He pursed his lips. "That should do. Now address the envelope."

They returned to find Jeremy's painting propped on a chair. Jeremy had not seen it for months and was pleasantly surprised by his skill. Elly stood back, studying the canvas. Two slender redheads, similar as bookends, somewhere between girlhood and womanhood, smiled back at her.

Jeremy handed Isabelle a large envelope containing Elly's letter. Isabelle had written her own note, which she placed in the envelope. She then addressed it to her brother, and handed it to Rory. "Mr. Cook, kindly take this to my footman. Tell him it is an urgent message for Edward Hereford."

Rory bowed slightly. "Yes, Lady Richfield."

Jeremy returned to his seat and sat back, rubbing his tired eyes. He smiled at Katherine. She blinked and smiled back.

Isabelle enjoyed watching their silent communication. Her gaze drifted back to Elly, still studying the painting. "So, Miss Fielding, there are the twins. Granted, that fine painting is an artist's copy of another artist's interpretation, but…"

"You are correct, Lady Richfield. I look very much like those girls. Their eyes are blue and mine are green, otherwise, we are quite the same." Her words were slightly over emphasized, as though she did not believe them. Jeremy did not believe them. Thin redheaded girls were as common as pigeons in Leicester Square.

Isabelle looked fondly at the canvas. "The sisters looked identical, but had totally different personalities. Even as a child, my mother loved plants and animals, biology and botany. She is a truly great herbalist. Her sister Caroline wanted pretty clothes and dolls. She eloped with a German Count when she was sixteen. It was a suitable match, so her parents were relieved. Caroline's first daughter was born within the year and given a German name we couldn't pronounce. It may have been Elisa." She exchanged glances with Elly. "Caroline's second daughter was named Bertha. My mother married much later, so Caroline's daughters were half-grown when I was born.

"Over the years, Mother tried to keep in touch with her twin, but Caroline and her husband traveled constantly. A few times a year, postcards arrived from exotic places. The day before my fifteenth birthday, mother received a letter from Caroline's daughter, possibly named Elisa, saying Caroline and her husband had been killed in a train wreck in Egypt. The other daughter Bertha had married an Englishman and was expecting a child. I have no idea what happened to her after that." She looked terribly sad.

Elly took a sip of her now cold tea. Her hand shook and she dribbled some down her front. Looking mortified, she clutched a serviette and tried wiping off the stain.

Isabelle smiled kindly. "No matter, Miss Fielding. Mr. Cook told me you have not been able to fetch your fresh frocks."

"No, Lady Richfield. Robert Dennison packed them in crates like the ones carrying his paintings. My crates are marked with a red X."

"Which gallery were they delivered to?"

"Gildstein."

"I'll send one of my footmen around tomorrow. Where should they be delivered?" She waited. No one spoke. "Well?"

Elly shrugged her shoulders. "You are very gracious, and I beg your pardon, but I am living at Mrs. Potter's boarding house, and…"

"That impossible shambles on Charles II Street?"

"Yes, ma'am."

Isabelle scowled. "Jerry, that place should be burned down. Surely Eric Bates can find his actors better lodgings."

Jeremy scowled. "Better, yes. Cheaper, no."

"I see."

Elly continued. "I share a room with two other apprentices. They do not have very nice clothes. They…"

Isabelle cut to the core. "They will steal your clothes."

"Yes."

"Then they must be delivered someplace else. All right, where?" Still, no one spoke. "Come on you lot, don't all talk at once. How many frocks are there?"

"Four, with accessories."

"How many can you safely guard at the boardinghouse?"

Elly thought for a minute. "There is an attic no one uses, so, perhaps, two."

"Very well. Tomorrow the boxes will be delivered to my house. At your leisure, come and collect whatever you like. I'll store the rest."

Elly swallowed hard. "Are you quite sure? You really are too kind."

"Not at all. I have three young daughters. A few extra frocks in the house will not even be noticed." Isabelle waved her hand, dismissing the subject.

The doorbell rang and Rory was shown back in. Isabelle turned her head. "Dispatched, Mr. Cook?"

"Yes, Lady Richfield." He nodded politely, and sat down. Evan took his toy soldiers and disappeared under the table.

Isabelle watched him go. "My brother should receive the packet on Tuesday. Miss Fielding's letter may not reach her father until Friday or Saturday." She calculated the days and laughed. "It will be a Christmas card he will not soon forget." She raised an eyebrow. "Now to the really intriguing matter: your parentage." She leaned toward Elly, and the girl shrunk back in her chair.

Jeremy wearily shook his head. "We are clutching at straws, Isabelle."

"Mr. Cook made that quite clear. Miss Fielding, my solicitor is a man of absolute discretion. With your permission, I shall have him look into the matter. He may find nothing, but I can see no harm in trying." Elly's shoulders tensed as she stared down at her spilled tea.

Katherine spoke softly. "Elly dear, if by chance your father is not related to you by blood, he may have no legal claim on you. Then you will be free to do as you please."

Elly forced out a hoarse whisper. "Thank you, Lady Richfield. I am very grateful."

Isabelle smiled. "Perhaps he can also discover if your mother left you an estate."

85

Katherine's eyelids were drooping, and Jeremy knew she longed to fall into bed. He would not let Elly leave the house without understanding that she could be carrying a child.

The clock struck nine and he put on a cheerful face. "Ladies and gentlemen, the hours pass. You ladies have lady business to discuss, so we gents bid you a pleasant good-evening. Katie, I will keep the chaps with me tonight and see you tomorrow for breakfast. Evan. Rory." He bent his head in Elly's direction, and lightly tapped his stomach.

Understanding his sign language, Katherine gestured to Isabelle that she should wait. Rory looked confused, but jumped to his feet. Evan emerged from under the table. After hasty farewells, Jeremy ushered the two chaps down the stairs, and closed the top door.

As soon as the men were gone, Katherine dropped her head into her hands. Isabelle slouched back into her chair. Katherine looked up with one eye. "Bless you, Isabelle. You're a saint."

"A saint?" Isabelle stretched and smiled. "I'll remind you of that the next time you're vexed with me."

Katherine laughed and shivered. "I'm cold, let's sit by the fire." They went into the drawing room. Isabelle helped herself to an easy chair. Katherine pulled Elly next to her on the sofa, put an arm around her waist, and hugged her affectionately. "You pulled off quite a feat, young lady."

Elly was startled. "I'm not sure what you mean."

Katherine chuckled, "My Jerry is not easily swayed. When Rory told me you were a runaway, I already pictured you on a train home."

"But, I would not have gone home." Elly sat tall. "Even if I had been forced onto a train, I would have gotten off again. I'll kill myself before going home." Her speech was calm and the older women were concerned. She continued in a quiet, matter-of-fact way. "We talked about that, Robert and I, what I could do if the theatre didn't take me. I have a few pounds saved. I would have found a boardinghouse and a position, any position."

Isabelle tilted her face. "Employment isn't that easy to find, and young girls need permission from their fathers before…"

"I would have worked as a skivvy, a pub girl, anything."

The older women exchanged looks, imagining this beautiful young innocent dragged into a brothel. Katherine smiled reassuringly and pushed loose hairs away from Elly's face. "Well, isn't it nice you don't have to. That's not to say a bed at Mrs. Potter's boardinghouse, or apprenticing with Jeremy O'Connell are particularly comfortable situations."

Elly's shoulders tensed. She whispered, "How do you know if you're going to have a child?"

Both women looked at her. Katherine answered softly. "Your monthly visits stop. After about the second month you begin to gain weight. You may feel ill in the morning."

Isabelle asked, "Are you expecting a child?"

"I don't know."

"When were you last with a man?"

"It was only once. Last Thursday."

"From your expression, I don't think you liked it."

She shook her head.

"Well, not liking it the first time seems to be the fate of most women. Fortunately, there are men who know how to do it. Make sure your next lover is experienced."

"I'll never have another." She spoke with disturbing finality, so Isabelle chuckled.

"What nonsense! You are beautiful, and sweet. You'll enjoy a bevy of handsome men." Elly stared up and Isabelle smiled kindly. "How long ago was your last monthly visitor? What day did it finish? Exactly."

Katherine and Isabelle watched tensely as Elly concentrated, calculating the days. "I think it was... No, I remember, it finished Thursday, last." She smiled and nodded. "Yes, I was pleased I had gotten it over with, before coming to London."

Both women looked grim. Isabelle spoke slowly. "So, your bleeding stopped on a Thursday, and your young man took you on the next Thursday?"

"Early Friday morning, actually. Yes, ma'am." She swallowed. "Is that bad?"

Trying not to frighten her more, Isabelle moved her head from side-to-side. "It could be."

Elly looked very upset, so Katherine took her hand. "It also may not be. We need to wait another three weeks and..."

"No." Isabelle's voice was quiet, but emphatic. "We do not need to wait. Jerry mentioned that I am skilled with herbs. I shall give you some. You simply make them into a tea. Drink a cup in the evening, the following morning, and again the following evening. Within the next twenty-four-hours, your bleeding will come and take away the beginning of any child. The whole business will be quickly finished and done. You're a clever girl and you'll do as I say. All right, dear?"

Elly's throat felt thick as she murmured, "Whatever you think best, Lady Richfield."

Katherine put an arm around her. "It's getting late, but I can't send you back to Mrs. Potter's. Would you like to spend the night?"

"Oh, may I? Yes, please!"

Chapter 9

Monday, December 21, 1903

The afternoon sky was a brilliant blue, dotted with thick, fluffy clouds. Katherine stayed home to write letters, while Jeremy, Evan, Rory, and Elly raced to Hyde Park. Bright sunlight warmed dozens of smiling people relaxing on benches and blankets. Evan and Rory went to fly a kite, as Jeremy spread a rough blanket over the brown grass. Elly sat on the edge, modestly tucking her long legs under her coat.

Jeremy watched bright kites soar overhead. "I love anything that flies. I am so jealous of the birds. Did you know that just last week, in America, two brothers actually flew an engine driven... I think they called it a 'Flyer'? I went up in a balloon once. It was marvelous."

"Weren't you afraid?"

"Terrified. That was part of the fun."

Since he was in a good mood, she dared to say, "Thank you for not sending me away."

He chuckled kindly. "No thanks are in order. Your arguments were highly convincing." He nodded toward Rory and Evan, and laughed as the boys clumsily bumped into each other. "You convinced me that you will be an asset to our company. It was all your doing." She stared with wide eyes, and he explained, "You are blessed with intelligence, beauty, and courage. Those are the makings of an actress."

She swallowed, listening intently.

"This was your first, and a vitally important lesson. You must always convince people that you are wonderful, especially when you do not believe it. Speak the words and they are half true. Speak them twice and they become true. Ours is a very hard profession. When we are out of work, we suffer until we find work. Once we find work, we suffer more. There are sadistic directors," he smiled impishly, "costumers who make us look fat, other actors who destroy our timing, stage pieces that fall on our heads, and critics who tell all the world that we are rubbish. If we do not believe that we are marvelous, no one else will."

She clutched her hands together, nervously shaking her head. "But I am not marvelous. You are over-kind to think me an asset before I have proven my worth, and we have acting class tomorrow. The other actors told me what it is like, and I know I will be dreadful." Bright tears lit her eyes, but as always, they did not run down her cheeks. The narrow vein in her temple pulsed as it had that day in the pub.

Jeremy was concerned. "Have you been told that you must not cry?"

She blinked the tears away. "My father and Sir John, my intended, forbid me to cry." She swallowed hard. "Robert Dennison believes that tears are necessary, sometimes even for men." Her voice cracked, a drop ran down her cheek, and the vein flattened.

"Well, points for Dennison in this one case at least. As an actress you will play tragic scenes, and I will expect you to cry buckets." He comically leaned into her and she laughed. "Elly, Elly, Elly... No one expects you to be marvelous tomorrow. Frankly, if you are still standing by the end of your monologue, the chaps will be impressed."

"What about the women?"

"The women, too. The girls will hate you, if they do not already."

"Peg hates me."

He laughed sardonically. "Small wonder."

"But why? I have done nothing to..."

"Oh, my dear. Are you actually that naïve?" He looked at her staring back with huge innocent eyes. "I believe that you are." He shook his head. "My dear, you are beautiful. Many men will fall in love with you for that alone, and many women will despise you for that alone."

"But I haven't done..."

"You do not have to *do* anything. Once you start playing roles, you..."

She sat up straighter. "Will I be playing roles?"

"I do not waste my time on anyone who is not capable. You know that Peg is in love with Rory."

Her mouth dropped open. "Oh no, sir. She hates him. At the boardinghouse they rowed terribly. She threw a tea-mug at him."

"Did she really? Well, he would not be able to distress her, if she did not care for him."

"I have heard that she..." She lowered her gaze.

"That she aborted a child? Yes. That is common knowledge, and to answer your next question: No, Rory was not the father. Did he bed her?

Repeatedly. The first weeks he was here, he could not get enough of her. Being the class of man that he is, he tired of her. Being the class of girl that she is, she still clings to him. Now that Rory fancies you, I imagine that Peg despises you both." He checked his pocket watch. "Nearly tea time. The good Lady Richfield expects us at 5:30. We had best be on our way."

Sir William Richfield's house was a block from Green Park on the corner of Piccadilly and Hamilton Place. At exactly 5:30 they appeared rosy-cheeked and hungry for high tea. The smiling butler answered the carved wooden door, festively decorated with holly and pine. "Good afternoon, Mr. O'Connell, Miss, Sir, Master Evan. Please come in."

Jeremy handed over his coat, hat, and kite. "Thank you, Smythe." A row of servants took their hats and coats.

A robust, "Hello all! Jerry, good to see you," came from Sir William Richfield. Middle-aged, tall, plump, and very jolly, he pumped Jeremy's hand.

"Good afternoon, Bill. May I present two of my apprentices, Elly Fielding and Rory Cook. You know Evan, of course."

"How-do-you-do? I see the theatre's future is in good hands. Well done, Jerry." He turned to Evan. "How are you, m' boy?"

"Very well sir, thank you. Is Lucy here?"

"She's upstairs with her mother, and yours. Oh, I'm supposed to send the young lady up to them." He turned to Elly. "Miss… um… sorry… mind like a sieve."

Elly laughed sweetly. "…Fielding. I'm sure your Lordship's mind is full of far more important things than the names of young girls."

A silly smile spread across Sir William's face and his eyes went out of focus. Jeremy was surprised and pleased. Perhaps Elly was not so naïve after all.

Evan grabbed Elly's hand. "I'll show you." He led her up the wide staircase.

Very shortly, the men were ushered into the west dining room. Isabelle, her pretty twelve-year-old daughter Lucy, Evan, Katherine, and Elly greeted the men. Elly had changed into a fresh dark-pink frock. Her hair was tied with a pink satin ribbon.

Happy calls of, "Mummy! Daddy!" came from seven-year-old Cindy, and four-year-old Bella. They raced first into Isabelle's waiting arms, then Sir William's.

Rory held Isabelle's chair. She sat gracefully while brushing her fingers over his hand. It was a slight gesture, but he caught his breath and stared into her smiling eyes. Coloring slightly, he sat next to Elly, and cut her a slice of game pie. "We need to eat. Tonight we're back at Potter's."

Isabelle looked up. "Mr. Cook, tell me about this infamous boardinghouse."

He raised an eyebrow. "There's not much to tell, Lady Richfield. Those who never had a dry roof in their lives think it's grand. Some of us find it a hell hole."

She shook her head. "How long have you lived there?"

"Year-and-a-half."

"An entire year-and-a-half?"

"Some have been there much longer."

"How does one get out?"

"Hilda Bates decides you're worth wages and puts you on salary."

Jeremy bellowed happily, "You won't have to wait much longer." Rory sat to attention and Jeremy beamed, "I'm sorry, my boy. I wanted you on salary for the Scottish Play. You will get wages for *The Tempest*. Just do me a favor and look surprised when Eric tells you."

"Thank you, sir. I certainly shall." Everyone cheered and applauded.

When the meal finished, the men and children went to the games room. Isabelle excused the ladies, and took them upstairs to her luxurious bedroom. The canopy bed was a masterpiece of embroidered silk, and Elly could not imagine falling asleep in such a museum piece.

A maid carried in a tray with a small tea pot, one cup, and saucer. She set the tray on a table, and curtsied. Isabelle thanked her, followed her to the door, and locked her out.

Katherine sat on the edge of a loveseat and Elly hovered near the door.

Calm and methodical, Isabelle walked to one of several wardrobes, unlocked a wooden door, removed a small apothecary's chest, and brought the chest to a table. She opened two small drawers, scooped a few dark twigs from one, powdery leaf fragments from the other, and put them into the teacup. When she carefully poured boiling water over the twigs, a musty aroma filled the air. "That needs to brew for a bit." She covered the cup with the saucer and sat back.

Elly's breathing was quick and shallow. "Must I do this?"

Isabelle looked her squarely in the eye. "No. But you would be very foolish not to." She took two small gauze sachets and carefully filled them with the herbs.

Elly tried again. "What if I'm not...?"

"Your bleeding will simply come earlier and stronger than usual. It's foolish to wait. I know. I waited... once. The second time, I did not. Here are two sachets, one for tomorrow morning, and another for tomorrow night." She went back to the wardrobe and found a parcel wrapped in brown paper. "These are fresh rags. On Wednesday you'll need plenty. By Thursday it should all be over." She smiled. "Like a bad dream."

Katherine stared at the floor. "Friday's Christmas," and looked at Elly. "Wednesday's your birthday."

Isabelle's eyes widened. "Is it really?"

Elly nodded solemnly.

"Which one?"

"Eighteen."

"Eighteen. So very young." Isabelle smiled sadly. "Not the way one envisions one's birthday." She placed a hand under Elly's chin. "You'll have to brew the other sachets yourself. Can I trust you to do that?"

Elly shook her head tearfully. "No." She looked to Katherine for support. Katherine's complexion had gone white. She shrugged noncommittally. Elly looked at the steaming tea, then at Isabelle. She clenched her jaw. "Yes!"

"Good girl." Sighing with relief, Isabelle took Elly in her arms, and held her for a long time. The girl's racing heart slowed, as she drew strength from the older woman. Isabelle released her, and handed her the teacup.

Staring at the murky brew, Elly recited, "*Romeo, I come! This do I drink to thee.*"

The older women laughed at Elly's humor and courage.

Without another word, Elly took a deep breath and drank the bitter potion.

Chapter 10

It was dark when Rory and Elly walked up Charles II Street toward Mrs. Potter's boardinghouse. She felt like Cinderella after midnight. The pumpkin had been left in a mansion at Hamilton Place and wicked stepsisters waited upstairs. Rather than racing to her rescue, Prince Charming Rory was counting the hours until he could move out. Looking up, she was relieved to see that the windows of her room were dark. Perhaps Meg and Peg were still away.

If she lived through tonight, tomorrow held three new adventures: 10:00 costume shop, 12:00 wig shop, 1:00 acting class. First thing tomorrow she would have to find boiling water and brew her dreaded elixir.

Rory carried a shabby suitcase Isabelle's maid found in a storage room. Inside were one of Elly's clean frocks and the package of rags. Elly wanted to run back to Isabelle, now. She wanted to be little Bella, hugged tight in her mother's arms. Rory put down the suitcase and took Elly's hand. "What happened tonight?"

"What do you mean?"

"Before tea, you were a butterfly. I thought Sir William was going to order you served on toast." She laughed nervously, and he pulled her closer. "After Lady Richfield took you upstairs, you were totally different. What happened?"

She shook her head, took the suitcase, and hurried into the house.

Peter, Mrs. Lynn, Lester, Todd, Meg, and Peg warmed themselves around the meager drawing room fire. They exchanged greetings, and Elly met Peg's icy glare. Hiding the suitcase behind her coat, she lit a candle stub, climbed to the attic, and left the case in a corner.

Back down stairs, the door to her room creaked as she opened it, tiptoed in, and shut it behind her. She planned to undress, hurry into bed, and pretend to be asleep when the other girls came up. The room was dark, but her candle flame easily lit her way to the wardrobe. A soft hiss made her jump. She looked around. "Hello?" All she could see were dark shadows. "Is anyone there?" She moved her candle, looking in all directions.

"*Hiss-s-s-s-s!*"

Elly froze. Her skin tingled with cold. "Who's there? ...Please! ...Is it Peg? ... I mean, Marguerite?" Shivering, she looked around again, then hurried toward the door.

The hissing voice was in front of her. "What in bloody 'ell you doin', Princess?"

Elly lurched back, her throat was in her mouth.

The voice seemed to be moving. "I cam up t' see 'ow you was makin' out, and you become invisible. Bloody enchantment i' was, Princess... Where y' been?... Eh?"

Elly couldn't see more than a few feet on either side. She could hardly breathe. "I can't see you. The light's very bad."

"The light's all righ'. I'm just invisible, like you." The voice was very close and Elly looked around frantically.

"That's Peg isn't it?" She tried to smile. "Marguerite?" There was no response. "That's your witch voice, isn't?" She turned in circles. "You were marvelous in the play." There was no sound, and her own voice crackled with fear. "I saw it twice... I didn't get a chance to tell you... You're a wonderful actress... Marguerite? ...Where are you? ...Why are you doing this?" She laughed nervously. "Isn't Hide-And-Seek a children's game? Is there another candle?"

A huge flame exploded in front of her face. She screamed and fell back onto the floor. Thick smoke filled the air and the stink of burning oil made her cough. All at once, four lit candles floated in midair. Peg was in the center -- like a dark goddess.

Seconds later, the door burst open. Rory rushed in, saw Peg surrounded by fire, and Elly on the floor.

Peg held out her arms and smiled. "Hello, Rory." Her diction was suddenly upper-class.

He ran to help Elly as Todd, Lester, and Peter hurried through the door. They all stopped dead, watching the unholy vision.

Peg forced a theatrical laugh. "Hello chaps! I've been showing Miss Fielding some of Jamie Jamison's Pyro-Magic. Do you want to watch the show?"

Elly stared straight ahead, her face deathly white. She felt herself being lifted up, and heard Rory say, "Get her out of here." Todd carried her downstairs. Lester followed.

*

Peter picked up a blackened torch. "Peg! You stupid fool! You could have burned the house down."

Rory ran to open the one unbroken window. A cold blast whirled the smoke in ghostly circles. He turned back and saw Satan's black-eyed mistress, surrounded by flames.

Peter said, "Come on, old chap, let's not make matters worse."

"Not to worry, Peter. I'm not going to kill her. Not just now." Rory's beautifully modulated voice made Peg gasp.

Peter rushed to him. "Rory boy, enough bad's been done tonight…"

"Not quite enough…"

The color drained from Peg's face. She stepped backwards, knocking over a chair and a jar of kerosene at her feet. It spilled on the floor and nauseating fumes filled the room. She threw back her head and smiled. "Why Rory, you look like a wolf tonight."

"And what are you?" He started toward her and Peter stepped between them.

"Come on Rory, boy. Keep your wits about you."

"Don't worry Peter. I have no intention of swinging from a rope in Newgate. Not for this piece of filth. Be a good chap and give us a bit of privacy."

Peg cocked her head. "That's right Peter. Be a good chap and leave a couple lovers to have their final quarrel." Batting her eyes at Rory, she put her foot on the overturned chair and raised her skirt above her knee.

Peter stepped back, his hands protectively in front of him. "You're both mad." He backed from the room and stumbled down the stairs.

Without taking his eyes off Peg, Rory crossed the room and shut the door. He started towards her and she ran around the other side of the bed. She spread her legs, casually rotating her hips. "Was I too much for you? Maybe you need virgins to prove what a big man you are." He continued towards her and she flattened herself against the wall. "I wasn't going to hurt the little bitch. I just wanted to scare her."

"Why? She's done nothing to you."

"Nothing! Is stealing a lover nothing?"

"A lover? We were never lovers. We fornicated like a couple of dogs."

"Is that what it was to you? To me it was love!" She screamed out a sob, and sunk into a dejected heap. The four floating candles flashed murky shadows across the room. When she raised her head, Rory caught his breath. Her high brows had softened. The sharp creases around her lips puckered in a childish pout. Tears spilled down her cheeks. "Why dan' y' luv me anymore?"

Despite the cold, perspiration ran down Rory's back. "I'm sorry it went so wrong, truly... I am truly sorry... I never meant to hurt you. I was nineteen, a frustrated university boy. You were so pretty, so devil may care, so exciting. I loved it. But it wasn't love."

"I' was t' me."

He ran his fingers through his hair, collecting his thoughts. "Peg... what about Elly?

"Wha' about 'er?"

"She's done nothing wrong. Does she have to be punished, because I love her?"

Like a little girl, Peg sat up and crossed her legs under her. "Do y' really luv 'er?"

"Yes!" His heart raced. He was short of breath. "I've never felt like this about a girl, not ever." He gasped, amazed at his own words. "I would die for her." He glared at Peg. "Tonight, I almost killed for her."

Her eyes filled up again. "It's really over, i'nt it."

"It's been really over for a long time."

"An' I never knew i'." She shrugged her shoulders, stood up, and wiped her face with her skirt. "Well, there's nothin' fer me 'ere. Guess I'll go find me a bloke."

"Don't be stupid, it's too late, it's not safe."

She laughed. "All of a sudden 'e's worried if I'm safe?" She started to go and he caught her arm.

"You won't find a decent man at this hour."

"Well, if I'm filf, wha's the difference?"

"I'm sorry, I didn't mean it, I was angry. Just promise me you won't hurt Elly."

"I ain't promisin' you shit!" She ran past him, into the hall, and down the stairs. Grabbing her coat, she growled like a deranged tiger and charged out, into the night.

Rory hurried to the four floating candles. Up close he saw that they were suspended by threads attached to the ceiling. He blew them out, raced downstairs, and found Elly on the drawing room sofa, covered with a pile of coats. Lester knelt beside her, rubbing her hands.

Rory sighed, "Peg won't be back tonight."

Lester gave a twisted smile. "That's good news. But how do you know?"

"She's gone to find a bloke. If she comes back, it means she couldn't find one. She'll stay away, if she has to sleep in the street. How the hell did she learn Pyro-Magic? Jamie Jamison refuses to teach anybody."

Elly was barely aware of being carried to bed. Meg tucked her in, got in herself, and snuggled protectively. Mrs. Potter was right. It was warmer sleeping with someone else.

*

Peg left Mrs. Potter's boardinghouse, running at full speed. Sure no one was following, she took a minute to catch her breath, and read the street signs. She wandered a few more blocks, then made a beeline to the only place she was sure to find a hot meal and a clean bed. It was a half-hour's walk before she saw the dimly lit pub sign: THE PINK KITTEN.

Chapter 11

Tuesday, December 22, 1903

The morning air was crisp, the sky was blue, and Elly had a spring in her step. Refreshed after a good night's sleep, she put yesterday from her mind, and dove into today's adventures. She stopped at *The Actress and Villain* and asked Timmy for a cup of hot water. Taking her cup to a back table, she opened a sachet, and dropped in the herbs. The smoky aroma wafted up. "*Come, vial. What if this mixture do not work at all? What if it be poison?*" She shivered, grateful for Isabelle's packet of clean rags. Taking a deep breath, she stirred the herbs, let them settle, then swallowed the bitter tea in large gulps.

The stage-doorkeeper gave her directions upstairs to wardrobe. The large room had sparkling white walls and long windows. Bright sunlight shined through at sharp angles. Two long tables, one clean, and the other stacked with bolts of bright fabric, stood side-by-side. Racks of costumes from the two current productions stood against two walls. Elly walked to a third wall, covered with detailed watercolour costume designs. On one side were earth-tone sketches from *Macbeth* and contemporary designs for *The Magistrate*. On the other side were fantastically bright sketches for *The Tempest*. Walking from picture to picture, she marveled that this two-dimensional medium created an illusion of three-dimensional life and movement, then laughed at her observations. Robert Dennison was a good art teacher.

"Ah! You're Elly Fielding." A tall, very thin woman in a straight black frock stood in the doorway. Unnaturally black hair framed chalk-white skin. Enormous darkly painted eyes and blood-red lips all seemed to curve into a thin smile. Her imposing figure reminded Elly of the witch from *Snow White*. She was followed by a short, stout woman, wearing an oriental print swirling with purples and electric green. Her gray hair was wildly streaked with red. The tall woman's eyes sparkled. "I'm Veronica Wallace, costume designer. This is Connie Vickers, the wardrobe mistress."

Elly's throat felt dry. "Yes ma'am. I was told to report for duty."

"We won't have any piecework for apprentices until rehearsals for *The Tempest* begin, but I'm glad you're here." Both women looked Elly up and down. Veronica nodded in approval. "O'Connell chose well. You're taller than I'd like, but your shape is perfect." Connie nodded in agreement, then beamed at Elly, making her feel uncomfortably like a prize poodle.

Veronica motioned Elly over to a long table and opened a portfolio. "We can get measurements for your costumes. Come, look at these." She took out four magnificent water colours and laid them side by side. "Aren't they exquisite?" Four sensuous nymphs danced across the pages. They appeared to be naked, covered only by the flimsiest pastel gauze.

Connie took a note pad and slung a tape measure around her neck. "You can't wear a corset under these costumes, so we'll need to get your true measurements."

"Oh, yes, of course." Elly stood like a mannequin as the older women undressed and measured her. Connie called out numbers and Veronica wrote them down. They were finished in minutes.

Veronica watched Elly dress, and made notes. "Connie, how soon can we have her under-garment finished?"

"End of the week."

"Fielding!"

Elly snapped to attention. "Yes, Miss Wallace."

Veronica pointed to the rack of *Macbeth* costumes. "Take those down to the dressing rooms. The actors' names are inside."

"Yes, ma'am." Elly looked over the rows of leather boots, doublets, voluptuous capes heavy as wool blankets, and tin suits appearing to be steal-plated amour. She lifted a costume off the rack. It was much heavier than she expected. "I'll have to make a few trips."

She took two costumes and struggled out of the room. It took her fourteen gruelling trips, down-and-up the stairs, to deliver all the costumes. Her legs ached and her arms felt as if they would break off. *Who did this job before I arrived?* She needed to rest, but the clock was nearing 12:00. Soon she would be due in the wig shop. Her stomach growled and she banished the uncomfortable sensation. *I'll just have to last until Mrs. Potter's delicious bread and lard at 6:00.* A different sensation teased the lower part of her stomach. *It can't be. It's too soon.*

The wig shop was above Eric Bates's office and referred to as, the "peacock's nest." The only way up was a narrow spiral staircase. Elly heard tinny music as she climbed round and round, approaching the open door above. Inside, an elfin man used a tiny crochet hook to weave strands of white hair through a silken mesh. His short dark hair framed almond shaped eyes with extraordinarily long lashes. The room was small, and dozens of wigs stood in tight rows, three tiers high. A bowl of loose hair and a bowl of apples sat on the work table. He sang along with a phonograph:

"My Sweetheart's The Man In The Moon
I'm going to marry him soon,
'T would fill me with bliss just to give him one kiss,
But I know that a dozen I never would miss…."

He saw Elly, squealed, shot his arms in the air, and down again. "Miss Elly Fielding, come to see me!" She laughed and he giggled with delight. "I'm Eugene, the wig-master, but then I suppose Michael told you all about me."
Elly sat down. "No, I'm sorry."
The tinny, nasal voice on the phonograph droned on:

"…I'll go up in a great big balloon
And see my sweetheart in the moon,
Then behind a dark cloud where no one is allow'd,
I'll make love to the man in the moon."

Eugene fluttered both hands close to his face and let out a quick sigh. "Oh, my. It's so like the boy to forget his friends." Elly laughed again, but feared she was being rude. Eugene enjoyed it. "Michael thinks only of the lovely Sandra, and forgets poor Eugene." He sighed long and loud, making Elly giggle even more.
"I'm sorry, but I don't know who Sandra is."
"Don't know who Sandra is? The love of his life? What does the boy speak of then?"
She shrugged. "He hasn't talked much about himself."

He pointed a finger. "Well, you see, my beauty, it's like this: I have a huge flat and I let rooms. My lodger, the lovely Sandra, is presently on tour with the Pantomime. She'll be Miranda, in *The Tempest*. A while ago, Michael moved in to be close to her. Don't know why they bother paying for two rooms, if you get my meaning." He put his hand over his mouth and giggled like a school girl.

Elly felt herself blush. She liked this charming elf. "I was told to report to you for work." She glanced at his bowl of apples.

He caught her look, and handed her two. "I keep these for starving actors."

"Thank you very much." She started to take a bite, but stopped as Eugene nearly pounced on her head.

"Ooh, I must see that hair!" Lightning fast, he removed her hairpins and released the copper mass. It cascaded across his arms and he ran his fingers through the thick folds. She tucked the two precious apples into her bag, as he combed her hair and wound it in different shapes, making delighted squeaks with each new style. "Hello, what's this then?" He was suddenly serious.

"What is it? What's wrong?"

He looked at the right side of her face and examined the hair closest to her forehead. "You either have a devilish curling iron, or you've been standing too close to fires."

"What do you mean?"

"Your hair is singed, just on one side."

"Is it really?" She was alarmed. "Is it bad?"

"Not to worry, I can fix it in a jiffy." Shears and comb in hand, he deftly snipped the hair around her face. He painstakingly trimmed up, down, and across the bottom. When he finally stepped back, and she could finally turn and look in the mirror, she was thrilled.

"It's beautiful." The loose wisps that constantly fell in her eyes had been cut short, curling naturally into a soft frame around her forehead. He had woven a sort of crown around the back of her head and pinned a silk rose onto one side.

*

Jeremy O'Connell arrived at His Majesty's Theatre and was surrounded by nervous actors. He quickly learned that Peg had attacked Elly, and almost burned down the boardinghouse. Eric Bates was with

102

two policemen, so Jeremy leapt upstairs, three-at-a-time. He met the coppers on their way down. They confirmed what he already guessed. No one knew the whereabouts of Peg McCarthy.

The year before, Eric's house had caught fire. Since he had been enjoying Peg's sexual services, and forced her to have a back alley abortion, they suspected she had been to blame. Now, Eric feared a scandal. Jeremy feared a potential murderess was stalking his actors. He hurried into Eric's office and shut the door. Trying to keep their voices low, the words, "...burn the sodding house down... bloody whore... out of here, now!" still echoed throughout the corridors.

Jeremy flung Eric's door open and stomped into the hall. His face was flushed, his eyes blazing. He stopped and stared. Eugene the wig-master and Elly Fielding calmly sat on the upstairs landing. "Elly, are you all right?"

"Yes sir, I'm fine." She came down to his level.

"You've cut some of your hair." He took her chin in his hand and carefully turned her face from one side to the other.

Eugene admired his fingernails. "I had to trim it, it was singed. She reported for work in the wig-shop, God bless her, after all she'd been through."

Jeremy bellowed at Eric, standing in the doorway. "Singed. Did you hear that?"

"Yes, I heard that."

He studied Elly's face. "Your right eyebrow is slightly singed, too." Embarrassed, she looked at the floor.

"All right, I'll deal with it." Eric pointed at Elly. "You look after that girl. I'll take care of the other."

Jeremy scowled. "Hardly the same thing." Eric went back inside and slammed the door.

Elly looked up shyly. "Please sir, who told you?"

"Everyone, actually." She looked distressed and he stared down at her. "This isn't something that should be kept quiet. Surely you don't think anyone faults *you* in any way?"

"No, sir."

"You're sure you're all right?"

"Yes sir, really." She broke into a smile. "Thank you for your concern."

He looked up. "Thank you, Eugene." The wig-master posed a hand on his chest, and dipped into a half curtsy. "Miss Fielding, I will see you in class."

A few minutes later Elly entered the rehearsal hall. She was rushed by people asking about Peg's attack. The clock struck 1:00 and Jeremy entered, casually strolling to the front of the room. All conversation ceased as a dozen actors scattered like nervous pigeons perching in three rows of chairs, arranged as the audience. Jeremy looked over the assembly and someone whispered, "Bli'me, 'e's in a good mood."

With a slight smile, Jeremy announced, "Ladies and gentlemen, I feel secure in saying that ours is the finest acting ensemble in Britain today. I am very proud, and I thank you." A dozen mouths fell open. "From my colleagues of many years…" He looked around the room, "Mr. Anderson, Miss Cushman, Mr. Moran, to the very newest of my young apprentices, you are a remarkable group of talented, industrious artists. I feel blessed to have you all in my company, at His Majesty's Theatre."

Someone started to applaud, and the whole room was quickly laughing, whistling, and clapping. As they quieted, he continued. "With luck, the fantastically talented Herbert Beerbohm Tree will extend his American tour, and we will be allowed to remain in his glorious edifice. If not," he raised both hands in a questioning gesture, "we will need to find a new theatre."

"Now -- Miss Stewart informs me that I was less than friendly during rehearsals for The Scottish Play." The actors broke into smiles and a few brave souls even laughed out loud. "In all likelihood, I will be no less unpleasant once we start rehearsals for *The Tempest*." The response was serious groans. "Much to my discontent, Miss Stewart will not be playing Miranda. However, I will rely heavily upon her as my general assistant, dramatic coach, and possibly a calming influence for the star."

The female baritone of elderly character actress Nancy Cushman boomed, "Hear! Hear!"

Other actors chuckled, and Jeremy bowed slightly. "Now, I have been watching understudy rehearsals for The Scottish Play and I am impressed." He looked at Owen. "Mr. Freeman."

He caught his breath. "Sir?"

"Your Macbeth is magnificent."

He exhaled. "Thank you, sir."

Jeremy raised an eyebrow. "Rest assured, you will never go on." This time the room exploded with laughter, and it took several minutes for everyone to settle down. Jeremy smiled and clapped his hands. "So ladies and gentlemen, to the business at hand. Mr. Moran, the list of scenes for today, if you please." Donald's impish face lit up under his bowl of thick gray hair. He stood to his full five-feet and handed Jeremy a slip of paper. "Very well. Who would like to begin?"

"Here, sir!" Lester shot up from the back row and Todd tried to pull him down. Lester grabbed his ear, whispering, "Get up you fool. Let's do it while he's in a good mood. You don't want to follow Owen or Michael do you?" Lester pushed Todd from his chair, and over three other actors, toward the stage area.

Jeremy sat at a small table, down-stage-right. He read from the paper. "*Two Gentlemen of Verona*, Launce and Speed, all right gentlemen, if you please."

Elly did not know this play, but from the first lines it was obviously one of Shakespeare's silly servant scenes. The young men were doing well and the audience enjoyed them. Jeremy sat back, crossed his arms, and put a finger over his lips.

When the scene finished, he sat up. "All right. Gentlemen, take a seat." Lester and Todd sat facing him. "Why do you suppose Shakespeare wrote these two characters?"

They looked at each other. Lester offered, "They give the audience needed information."

"Yes, Mr. Reid, that is true, but even for Shakespeare, that information reaches the audience remarkably slowly. Any other ideas?"

Todd raised a very long, tentative finger. "Because they're funny?"

"Thank you, Mr. Sinclair. On the nose. They are *supposed* to be funny. Shakespeare has handed us two clowns. You have handed back prettily spoken, vapid words."

Almost imperceptibly, the entire audience leaned back, and held its breath.

"This is Shakespeare, lads. Not the..." He clenched his jaw, fighting back an expletive, "... the Bible! Every word is not sacred. The two of you are natural clowns. I see you clowning backstage, in the pub, on the bloody street. Go! Start it again."

This time, Lester smiled wickedly and snapped out his lines, teasing Todd with a letter. Frantic to get the letter, Todd used his height and long arms, grabbing for the letter around Lester's short arms and round stomach. He put one large foot over the other, tripped himself, and fell on his face. The audience roared with laughter.

Jeremy stopped them. "Yes! Better! Bring it back next week. Who is next?"

"Here sir!" Owen and Rory stood up.

Jeremy checked his paper. "*Romeo and Juliet*, Mercutio and Romeo, Mr. Moran, you're reading Benvolio?"

Donald smiled. "Yes, sir."

"Very well, gentlemen."

Elly had thought Jeremy's critique of Lester and Todd was hard, until she saw the difference his few words had made. The moment Rory and Owen began, her heart beat faster. She believed Rory was lovesick Romeo, but she was in love with Mercutio.

When they finished, Jeremy asked the actors to sit. "Mr. Cook. What is the name of this play?"

Rory hesitated, "Well... *Romeo and Juliet*, sir."

"Mr. Freeman, what is the name of this play?"

Owen put his elbows on his knees. He started laughing, "*Mercutio*?"

Jeremy laughed full out and some of the others joined in. "Mr. Cook."

"Sir."

"You were absolutely believable. Your intentions were clear and simple and I can find no fault, except that you disappeared." Rory flushed. His brow creased, and he watched Jeremy, memorizing every word. "Mr. Cook, the fault lies partially with Shakespeare, partly with Mr. Freeman, but largely with you. We can never know why The Bard chose to make a secondary character so dynamic. Not only is Mercutio more charming than Romeo, he also gets to die violently in a sword fight. When I was very young I toured as Romeo. The actor cast as Mercutio was more experienced than I, easily stole focus, and made my life hell. I learned a great deal, and Simon Camden has been one of my best friends ever since."

Reverential murmurs came from the crowd. Owen asked, "Sir, is Mr. Camden still touring America?"

"I believe so." Jeremy turned back to Rory. "Mr. Cook, as a junior-actor, you naturally defer to a senior-actor." He pointed a finger. "Don't do it. Not if you are the star. How do you feel about Mercutio's taunting?" Rory shrugged, so Jeremy pointed to Lester. "How do you feel when Mr. Reid taunts you?"

Lester chuckled and Rory clenched his jaw. "I hate it."

"With that in mind, gentlemen, please begin again."

The scene was totally different. Rory took stage and challenged Owen with every line. Owen enjoyed the stronger opponent, was able to create more variety and excitement. Elly was amazed at the difference. The scene ended and the audience applauded.

Jeremy nodded his approval. "Good. Bring it back next week."

Owen and Rory smiled at each other as they returned to their seats.

"Who is next?"

The booming bellow of Nancy Cushman rang out, "Come along Michael, let's take our med'cin." The audience knew this actress's comic genius and chuckled in anticipation.

Three pleasant hours flew by. At 4:20 Jeremy said, "Time for one more monologue. Miss Fielding, if you please."

Elly looked as if she were going to faint. Stumbling out of the back row, she staggered in front of the other actors, stared at Jeremy, and frantically blinked back nervous tears. She took a moment and looked into the imaginary afternoon sky. With Juliet's words, she begged the sun to hurry across the sky, allow night to fall and bring her lover. Elly's frustration with the never ending speech changed romantic longing into something different.

"Gallop apace, you fiery-footed steeds,
Towards Phoebus' lodging:....
When she recited, "*And learn me how to lose a winning match,*
Play'd for a pair of stainless maidenhoods:...." she looked shocked.

By the end of the monologue, Juliet's words begged her lover to come quickly, but Elly's expression commanded him to stay away. The confused audience applauded kindly. Elly sat stiffly in front of Jeremy, waiting for his critique.

He placed a finger over his lips. "Unusual interpretation, Miss Fielding." For a moment their eyes met. Jeremy knew how confused Elly felt about her real lover, and how confused her Juliet felt about her pretend lover.

The clock struck 4:30. "Next week we will begin with Miss Fielding. Thank you, ladies and gentlemen. I will see some of you tonight, on stage. To the rest, I wish you a pleasant evening." He made a slight bow and the class applauded.

That evening, Jeremy sat by the stove in his dressing-room. His door was half-open, allowing a soothing breeze to flutter through. His silk dressing-gown felt wonderfully soft, the tobacco in his long-stemmed pipe tasted sweet, and an entertaining novel made him smile. *The Wonderful Wizard of Oz* was a newly published story for children. He knew it could become a wonderful play. He turned a page, glanced up, and saw Elly Fielding. The poor girl struggled into the quick change room under the weight of several heavy costumes. Her dreadful job was assigned to the newest apprentice of either gender. She hung the clothes and waited at the end of the hall.

Jeremy lightly called, "Do come in, Miss Fielding." She looked as if her bones were melting, as she shuffled into his dressing-room. He offered her a chair.

"Thank you, sir. I hope I'm not intruding." She sat down, exhausted. "You were very kind to me in class. I didn't think that you would be."

He blinked like a contented cat. "I was not kind. That is not my style."

"Please help me." Tears filled her eyes. "I was dreadful this afternoon. I am so embarrassed. I don't know if you want to bother, but I want to learn so much. Please help me." Tears rolled down her cheeks and she quickly wiped them away.

He closed the door and returned to his seat. His pipe had gone out but he continued to chew on it. "You were not dreadful. Quite the contrary. As I said, your interpretation was unusual. You used the present-theatrical-reality of your own, very real fears, and put them behind the words. I enjoyed watching you, which is more than I can say for everything that was presented."

Her tears dried as she listened to his every word.

"You need a vocabulary of emotions you can draw on, like you would draw books off a shelf, and like a book, each emotion needs chapters,

108

variations. You did *not* want Romeo to come." He put his head back and laughed. "'...*and every tongue that speaks but Romeo's name speaks heavenly eloquence?'* You made '*heavenly eloquence*' sound as if it were horse manure." She cringed and he held up a hand. "It is all right. That was what Elly felt about Romeo ...or more probably, Robert Dennison, at that moment."

Confused and embarrassed, she stared at the floor.

He smiled fondly. "Now, I shall teach you how to access the appropriate emotion, at the appropriate time." He touched his chest with the pipe stem. "That is my job."

"Can you do that?" He glared and she panicked. "I don't mean, 'Can you do that?' I know you can teach it, but am I clever enough to learn it?"

"Without question."

"Truly?" She bit her lip. "When can we start?"

He laughed. "We can start right now if you don't mind working while I make up."

"Oh, yes, please! That would be wonderful."

There was a knock on the door. " 'alf hour, Mr. O'Connell."

"Thank you!" He turned to the mirror and put a towel around the neck of his dressing gown. With two fingers, he reached into a pot of greasepaint, took enough to fill the palm of his hand, rubbed it into a soft mush, and spread it over his face. "You must be clean with one set of feelings before you can move on to another. Why did you want Romeo to stay away?"

She looked at her hands and whispered, "I was afraid for Juliet. She doesn't know what it's going to be like."

"What does she think it is going to be like?"

"She thinks it is going to be wonderful."

"End of story."

Elly looked shocked but said nothing.

Jeremy mechanically applied line and shading, creating an exaggerated version of himself. "What are you feeling now?"

"I'm angry."

"Why?"

"Because it's not real, it's not like that the first night... the way Shakespeare wrote it. He was a man, he didn't know." Jeremy calmly

109

outlined his eyes with a charcoal stick and she shouted, "I've spoken with other women, it's never like that the first time!"

"You've spoken with every other woman in the world?"

"Of course not! What a stupid question!" Shocked at her outburst, she put her hand over her mouth.

He smiled. "Then, dear girl, in the case of Juliet, we must assume that she is one of the few lucky ones." He turned to look at her. "She pays a high price for her one night of bliss."

Elly swallowed a sob.

"Why are you so angry?"

"I don't know." She was almost crying.

There was a knock on the door. "Quarter hour, Mr. O'Connell!"

"Thank you! Ask my dresser to give me a minute."

He took Elly's hands, looked into her eyes, spoke slowly and softly. "Your first night was not like Juliet's. But you will have a second and a third." This time a whirlpool of tears filled her eyes, making her even more alluring and vulnerable. He laughed and shook his head. "You will have a hundred wonderful nights. Do not begrudge Juliet her one." Giving her a moment to compose herself, he stood up and called, "All right, Jeffers!"

The dresser came in and stopped dead. With the exception of Katherine, he had never found a lady in his master's room when the door was closed. Jeremy smiled to himself as Elly slipped from the room.

Chapter 12

Wednesday: December 23, 1903

"*O true apothecary*! *Thy drugs are quick*." Elly doubled over, collapsing on the backstage stairs. She curled into a ball, trying to ease the stabbing pain in her belly. That morning she had stuffed her under-drawers with rags, but they were not enough to absorb the blood gushing between her legs. Afraid of staining her skirt, she pulled it up around her waist, and braced herself on the hard wooden stairs. It was only 12:30, and none of the actors had arrived. In preparation for the matinee, she carried newly mended *Macbeth* costumes from the costume shop to the dressing rooms. They lay below her, in a mangled heap. Everything went white, then black.

She opened her eyes and lurched back in fright.

Peg McCarthy stood over her. "Dan worry. I ain't gonna 'urt y'. Y' been 'urt enough, by the look o' yer."

Elly sat up, horrified at the large red stain between her legs.

"'oo made y' do this, then? Can't a been nobody 'ere. Y' ain't been 'ere long enough." Elly was in a cold sweat, every fiber in her body screaming she should run away. She tried to stand and collapsed back down on the steps.

Peg whispered. "I wanted to keep mine. Bates wanted it gone, so it got gone. Did y' want yours?"

Elly shook her head.

"Well, yer a'righ' then. At least y' will be." Peg went down a few steps and gathered the costumes. "I'll take these. Used t' be my job anyway." Small as she was, she effortlessly carried them down stairs.

Elly was frantic to be gone by the time Peg returned. The pain in her belly stopped, leaving a dull ache between her legs. Her head began to clear. She heard the stairs creak and braced herself for Peg's return.

"Got any clean linen?"

Elly blinked her eyes. "Yes. I washed them yesterday. They should be dry. I hid some clean rags in the washroom."

"Come on, then." Peg practically lifted Elly off the step. "Can y' walk?"

Still holding her skirt away from her bloody underclothes, Elly took some deep breaths, nodded, and followed Peg down three flights of stairs. They could hear some of the crew, but fortunately saw no one.

Elly went into the washroom and closed the door. When she looked around, Peg was gone. After peeling off her bloody underclothes, she filled a basin with cold water, and put her rags, drawers, slip, and stockings to soak. The insides of her legs were covered with blood. Still dizzy, she slowly cleaned herself, pulled on the fresh underclothes, and stuffed in the rest of Isabelle's clean rags. The soiled linens rinsed easily and she carelessly tossed them over a drying rack. Bracing herself on the banister, she dragged herself back upstairs.

*

Before the *Macbeth* matinee, bloodstains were found on the backstage staircase. No one knew where they came from, but everyone suspected Peg McCarthy was involved. She had not signed in, and her understudy went on as the Second Witch.

At 6:00, Katherine Stewart and Jeremy O'Connell finished an early tea in front of the stove in his dressing-room. They had another performance at 8:00, so they still wore dark make-up, but no wigs. An outsider would have found them a ridiculous looking pair, but cast and crew passed by Jeremy's open door, seeing nothing unusual. He put a cigarette to his lips, yawned, and stretched. "Nap time, Katie."

"Not for me." She recited, "'Someone's sleeping in my bed,' said the mother bear."

"Who's sleeping in your bed, then?"

"Elly, poor dear."

"Since when do you let apprentices sleep in your dressing-room? Is she ill? She was fine last night."

"This afternoon she was wrecked and exhausted."

"What from, for heaven's sake? We're not even in production."

"From dislodging what may have been a child."

"What!" Horrified, he glared at her.

She glared back. "Your wish has been fulfilled. If she *was* with child, Isabelle's herbs have done away with it. She came to me after it was over. I fed her, put her to bed, and she's still asleep, or she was when we went to the greenroom. I left her some more food, just now."

Horrified, he relaxed his throat muscles enough to ask. "The girl is well, then?"

She held up her arms in a dramatic storybook fashion. "Let - us - go - and - see."

Moments later, Katherine knocked on her own dressing-room door, pushed it open, and smiled to see Elly finishing her supper. She quickly stood up, almost knocking over the chair. Reaching to calm her, Katherine put one hand on her shoulder and the other under her chin. "You look like yourself again. There's color in your cheeks, thank goodness. How do you feel?"

"I feel fine." She smiled. "I'm sorry I slept so long. You must want to rest."

"I do. And since you're awake, I will." Without ceremony, Katherine took a clean rag from her dressing table and covered the pillow on her cot, protecting it from the greasepaint on her face. She happily climbed onto the cot, pulled a quilt over herself, and closed her eyes.

Jeremy gently pushed Elly out the door. "'*Fairies, begone, and be always away.*"

*

That evening, Sir William and Lady Richfield watched *Macbeth* for a second time. After the final curtain, they left their box seats and easily found their way backstage through a pass door. Isabelle was about to knock on Katherine Stewart's door when she noticed Elly hanging costumes in the quick change room.

She peered through the doorway. "Elly, dear. Is it over?"

Elly stood proudly. "Yes, ma'am. I kept my promise."

"Good girl." She went inside and closed the door. "Was there a lot of pain?"

"Only for a few minutes. It was over very fast." Elly looked at Isabelle with absolute trust. Her sweet vulnerability made Isabelle want to shield her from the world.

"Thank goodness." She touched Elly's cheek. "Dreadful as that was, it's finished, and you can get on with your life. You've been through more in a few days than some people go through in a lifetime. I'm very proud of you."

"Thank you. You're so terribly kind." Elly's huge eyes were full of love, and fast breaths pushed her thin ribcage in and out. Isabelle looked at her waistline. Like any mother examining her child, Isabelle pushed the girl's hands away and felt her waist. "Your corset is actually loose."

"I don't know why I bother to wear one. I've always been thin." Embarrassed, she pulled away. "At the boardinghouse, there isn't very much food."

"Well, you certainly won't be going hungry again. Whether you're related to me, or not, I must do something to change your circumstances. My solicitor's people are checking your background. We should know something in a few days. Oh, I nearly forgot." She reached into her bag and pulled out a small bundle wrapped in a handkerchief. "My maid found this in one of your boxes."

Elly unwound the handkerchief, stopped and stared. It was the clay figurine of Kate, her long copper hair and blue costume, bright and smooth under heavy glaze.

Isabelle watched with interest. "She looks like you."

"It is me, in a costume from a school play. Thank you so much for finding this. I thought it was lost forever."

"Did Robert Dennison make it?"

Elly smiled and nodded.

Isabelle hesitated, then pulled her into a chair and sat down next to her. "Tell me about him."

Relieved and grateful, Elly told Isabelle every detail of the unorthodox relationship with her art-master. When she came to the terrible misunderstanding, the night before she left for London, Isabelle closed her eyes and shook her head. "That poor man."

Elly's mouth dropped open. "That poor man? What about me?"

"You child, were dumb ignorant, like most young women. We learn, and get over it. He, by the sound of it, did everything right, and it still turned out wrong." She leaned forward, speaking slowly. "Let me make sure I heard you correctly: You were both in your night clothes. You willing lay on your back, on the floor. He knelt in front of you, then *stopped* to ask if you wanted it?"

Elly nodded. "He asked twice."

"Twice!" Isabelle's eyes were like saucers.

114

Elly nodded, nervously stroking the figurine. "I thought he was going to touch me with his hand, like he had in the grotto."

"Oh, dear." Isabelle stood and stretched.

Elly cringed. "I know it was wrong of me to want it."

"No, it was not wrong. Every woman wants to be touched, in all manner of ways... after we finally learn to do it properly." She rubbed her brow. "I'm looking forward to meeting this painter of yours."

"You are? Even after he..."

"After he, what? If you've told me the truth, I can't fault him at all. Granted, in the conventions of our society, a school-master shouldn't even speak privately with a female student, but neither of you are conventional." She tilted her head with a surprised chuckle. "Have you any idea how extraordinary this man is? You have actually stumbled across a man who is talented, attractive, potent, and chivalrous. You have found a prince." She saw the girl's overwhelm, and her heart ached. "You need a long rest in a good bed. I'll tell Bill you're coming home with us tonight. We're giving a ball tomorrow night and dinner Christmas day. Don't worry about clothes. The house is full of anything you might need. I'll see if your beau wants to join us as well."

Elly sat up, surprised. "I don't have a beau."

Isabelle chuckled. "Rory thinks he's your beau."

"He's not. I'm fond of him, but..."

"Oh, I forgot something else." She opened her bag and handed Elly a small box. "Happy birthday. Kathy found this for you. It's from the two of us."

"I thought everyone had forgotten." Thrilled, Elly opened the box. "Oh, Lady Richfield. This is too beautiful." Inside lay a small brooch made from tiny, exquisitely carved, comedy and tragedy masks. The masks were burnished gold and the ribbons were sparkly diamond chips. Isabelle pinned it to Elly's rumpled pink collar.

Chapter 13

Thursday, December 24, 1903

Jeremy and his valet Max spent most of the next day chopping and stewing in preparation for Christmas dinner. The menu would be a succulent goose stuffed with sweetmeats, surrounded by roast potatoes and a sea of vegetables. There would be three kinds of wine, fresh rolls, giblet gravy, and a very rich Christmas pudding.

Jeremy always enjoyed preparing holiday meals, but this was to be the most important meal of his life. After the main course, before Max brought out the flaming pud', he intended to propose to Katherine. After twenty years of pretend marriage and fatherhood, he wanted to make it real and legal.

He planned to clear out Stephen's belongings, take down the wall between his bedroom and the guestroom, and make a master bedroom he and Katherine could share, every night. Evan would finally have all his belongings in one large room, the way he wanted them. Katherine disliked ostentatious jewelry, so Jeremy had purchased an exquisitely cut, but modest, diamond ring.

Not trusting himself to find the appropriate words, he borrowed Shakespeare's fourteenth sonnet for his proposal speech. He had memorized it as a boy, knew it as well as his own name, but silently repeated the words over and over, as a kind of prayer:

"Not from the stars do I my judgment pluck…
…But from thine eyes my knowledge I derive…"

Anticipating her loving tears, as he placed the ring on her finger, and Evan's rapture that his parents were finally marrying, Jeremy was happier than he ever remembered.

All too soon, it was time to dress for Isabelle's Christmas Eve ball. He left Max to finish in the kitchen, hurried through a bath, tossed on a dress suit, and met Katherine by the door. They took a hansom to the corner of

Piccadilly and Hamilton Place, arriving promptly at nine o'clock. The road was filled with Lord Richfield's footmen helping guests from carriages, across the sidewalk, and up the few steps into the house. In the foyer, another army of servants carried away coats and hats, served champagne and mulled wine.

Knowing that Isabelle's guests admired actors when they were on the stage, but considered them to be social riffraff, Katherine and Jeremy dressed very conservatively. He still looked stunning, clothed like any other man in conventional white-tie-and-tails. Katherine matched him in a simple but very elegant black-satin gown, long satin gloves, a double string of pearls, a matching bracelet, and earrings. Her only colorful item was a fresh holly broach. She wore just enough makeup to accentuate her translucent eyebrows, eyelashes, and the classic contours of her perfect face. Her honey-blond hair was swept up in an elegantly simple French twist. Many of Isabelle's other guests were society matrons wearing bright rouge and gaudy gowns. Jeremy had never felt prouder to have Katherine on his arm. Happily imagining her wearing his diamond ring, he moved her through the crowded foyer and heard:

"Kathy!"

Jeremy froze, horrified. The voice was unmistakable.

"Simon?" Katherine turned, frantically looking for the voice. She spotted him at the end of the room and hurried through the glittering guests. Jeremy was close at her heels, as she sped into a clear corner and the open arms of Simon Camden.

Heart pounding, fists at his sides, it was all Jeremy could do not to sock Simon. This was to be his Christmas alone with Katherine and Evan. Simon was not invited. In fifteen years, Simon had never arrived in London without giving Katherine weeks of warning. Also, he had never arrived looking this good. Simon was a road rat. He always appeared at her door with greasy hair, filthy clothes, and a half-week's growth of beard. His first days back, he had visited his barber, his tailor, and boot-maker and, by the end of the week, he became the stunning specimen he was right now.

Shorter than Jeremy, but still taller than most men, forty-two, and athletically built, Simon oozed charm. His thick golden hair was streaked with glossy silver, beautifully cut, and combed back, just touching his shoulders. Since he was not currently on the stage, he had grown a finely

117

manicured beard to frame his high cheekbones. An elegant moustache curved to match the delicate curve of his brows. His forehead was high, his nose was straight, and his gray eyes were laughing. His dress suit fit like a glove. His patent-leather slippers gleamed and his nails were buffed. For a split second Jeremy hoped Simon had fallen in love with some other woman. When he spun Katherine around, then kissed her passionately, that hope dissolved.

Katherine laughed with pleasure. "We thought you were in New York." She lovingly stroked his cheek, "I was so worried when your letters stopped coming."

"It's a long story. I've missed you."

"Oh, certainly." She laughed as he held her tight, kissing her again.

Longing to yank them apart, Jeremy clenched his fists and waited for the interminable kiss to end. When Simon finally came up for air, he turned his head and did a double-take. A vision of loveliness slithered through the crowd. He smiled hungrily. "Who is this Grecian goddess?"

*

Elly Fielding had arrived, excited and breathless, in an exquisite green-velvet gown. Youthful styling, and a stiff corset, molded her boyish figure into a shapely hourglass. The scooped neckline exposed the pristine white flesh of firm young breasts. A small gold theatre-mask broach was perfectly displayed near her cleavage. Her light-copper hair was swept up, with one long curl pulled cunningly over one naked shoulder. The slightest touch of charcoal accentuated her pale eyebrows and lashes, making her large green eyes appear even brighter.

Jeremy guessed that Isabelle's dressmaker had worked through the night. He offered his hand. "My dear, you are a vision." He bowed from the waist, lifting her gloved fingers to his lips. She lowered her eyes and curtsied. "Simon, may I present one of my apprentices, Elly Fielding? Miss Fielding, this is Simon Camden."

Elly looked faint as Simon stepped forward, slowly looking her up and down. "This is an apprentice? Things have certainly improved." Rather than bending toward her, he took her hand and pulled her toward him. They were nearly touching and her cheeks burned like fire. "You can still blush?" Smiling seductively, he brushed her fingers against his lips. "How lovely, you've not been jaded." Looking very uncomfortable, she jerked her hand away. He held it tight.

Katherine came to her rescue. "Simon, let the girl alone." She gently broke his hold.

He swung Katherine into another embrace. "I missed you, and I can't believe you're still mated to this old pouf."

At that, even Jeremy laughed. Katherine threw him a kiss. "You brought us together, all those years ago. Jerry is still the best thing going."

Feeling himself grow an extra two inches, Jeremy almost did not care when Simon moved his lips over hers, crooning, "You've been all over the world, in my mind."

A familiar voice croaked, "Mistletoe works, I see."

"Bernard!" Simon let Katherine go and extended his hand. "How long has it been?"

"You look well, my friend. The Americas agree with you." George Bernard Shaw shook Simon's hand, then Jeremy's, and kissed Katherine's cheek. "I'm not sure you all know Janet Achurch, and her husband Charles Carrington."

Simon took Janet's hand and bowed to kiss it. "Dear Lady, the fates have never allowed us to play in the same city at the same time. It is a tragedy that I have missed both your *Doll's House*, and your *Candida*."

Bernard Shaw looked around the vast hall. "Anymore of you thespian lot here tonight?"

Katherine pointed to a balcony. "I spotted Maurice Barrymore and his crowd when we first arrived."

Elly looked up and caught her breath. At the center of the grand staircase stood Rory Cook. Very handsome, with freshly cut hair and perfectly tailored evening-clothes, he leaned casually against the banister and chatted with three plain young women. They stared adoringly, and he enjoyed their attention.

Bernard Shaw and the others splintered into small groups.

Elly excused herself and slithered through the crowded hall. Simon watched her go.

Katherine smiled. "There's a young man on the stairs."

Simon squinted, trying to see across the wide hall. "Ah yes, good-looking blond chap. Short – one of yours?"

"Another apprentice, Rory Cook."

"In my day apprentices were poor."

Jeremy chuckled. "They are poor as church mice. Not a bean between them. Isabelle's taken a fancy and made them her dress-up dolls."

Simon nodded. "Good for them. That girl's an extraordinary beauty, what are you going to do with her?" Jeremy smiled suggestively and Simon sputtered, "All right, Jerry, I know what you're *not* going to do with her. More fool you. Can she act?"

"Not yet, but her instincts are marvelous."

"How old is she?"

"Eighteen, yesterday. Come on you lot, I'm famished."

Jeremy squeezed through clumps of genial partygoers. He slithered into the drawing room. Gleaming silver chafing dishes brimmed with stuffed lobster, thin slices of lean beef, glazed pheasant, roast potatoes, sautéed vegetables, and hot rolls. When he looked back, Katherine and Simon were gone. He cursed himself, guessing Simon had whisked her off to a secluded spot.

Rory sneaked up beside him. "This looks just like tea at Mrs. Potter's." Elly giggled over his shoulder and filled her small plate with socially polite, tiny helpings.

Hearing Isabelle's sparkling laugh, they turned and stared. "Jerry darling!" She flashed a brilliant smile. Her exquisite purple satin gown was trimmed with velvet and rustled as she walked. She wore an amethyst tiara, matching earrings, bracelets, and a wide choker, drawing attention to her smooth bare shoulders and full breasts. Her electric blue eyes reflected the violet from her gown. "Gentlemen, please do me a kindness."

Rory rushed to serve. "Yes, ma'am, anything at all."

Isabelle touched his cheek with gloved fingers and he looked like he was going to faint. "Rory dear, my ballroom is occupied by an abundance of ladies."

His smile faded. "At your service, Madam." He downed his glass of champagne and hurried away.

Isabelle whispered, "Jerry, be a darling. After you've had something to eat, dance with some of my poor wallflowers."

"Good grief, Isabelle! Are you serious?"

"Please!" Squeezing his arm, she looked up with pleading eyes, winked at Elly, and swooped away.

120

Jeremy helped himself from the buffet table as a young man rushed toward him. "Mr. O'Connell. What a pleasure. I saw *The Magistrate*. It was just great." His dark-blue eyes gleamed. "I'm Sam Smelling, freelance journalist, currently on assignment from the *New York Dramatic Mirror*. My column's called: Sam Smell, The Man With The Nose For News."

Jeremy looked down his nose. "Ah, yes... Smelling, the journalist. Isabelle mentioned meeting you in New York. Something in connection with horse racing, I believe."

Sam nodded jovially. "Good memory. I was investigating at one of the tracks." Suddenly noticing Elly, he shivered comically. "Oh, sorry. Um, I'm Sam Smelling." She politely shook his hand.

Jeremy sighed. "Mr. Smelling, allow me to present Elly Fielding, one of my appren..."

"I'm..." Elly interrupted, then looked caught. Mouth half-opened, she glanced between the two men.

Still holding her hand, Sam pretended to be deep in thought. "Just take your time. I know you'll remember who you are."

Elly laughed at herself and recited. "I'm Lady Richfield's cousin, visiting for the holiday."

Jeremy smiled to himself. It seemed Isabelle believed Elly really was family.

"Isabelle's cousin." Sam's easy smile made her relax. Neither tall nor short, he had a comfortable build and was just awfully pleasant. He pushed back his unruly dark hair. "That makes sense. Isabelle's the most beautiful woman in the world, and you're the most beautiful girl." His hair fell back over his eyes, making Elly smile. He laughed with her. "God gave me a great brain, but terrible hair. I think I'm part dog." They laughed together.

Jeremy finished his snack and pursed his lips. "Mr. Smelling, has our hostess conscripted you to dance with her surplus female guests?"

Sam looked surprised. "No, sir." He smiled sheepishly, "but then, I'm not much of a dancer."

"Lucky you. I shall pay my debt to friendship by finding the homeliest woman in the room and giving her one turn around the floor. After that I shall spend the evening as I please." He bowed and left.

*

When Jeremy finally returned, Elly and Sam looked like best friends, deep in conversation. "Are you two still here? I danced with my wallflower and was rewarded by partnering Isabelle and my lovely Katie. Now Simon has swept Katie away somewhere. Rory deserves a medal for all the Plain Janes he has partnered." He lightly commanded, "Miss Fielding, my next dance will be with you."

"Thank you, sir." She looked pleased, but nervous, as they said goodbye to Sam Smelling, and walked through the crowded foyer. Jeremy glanced out open French windows, into the shadowy garden.

Simon loped in. "Hello, you two." He posed melodramatically, raising the back of his hand to his forehead. "Kathy turned me down, once again."

Jeremy snorted, fluttering a hand. "If she ever said, 'Yes,' all your longing would disappear and your talent with it."

Simon pretended he had been socked in the stomach. "Ooh, that's a good one, Jerry. Points for you." His head came up under Jeremy's chin.

In a flash, Simon had Jeremy's arm pinned behind his back. Jeremy laughed, shouting, "Uncle!"

Simon laughed and rolled his eyes. "Jerry, can we go home? I'm not sure I can take any more of this ghastly party. Isabelle made me dance with her odious guests. They're all ninety-and-half-dead."

Jeremy laughed. "You were able to steal Katie away, and just where, pray tell, are you calling *home*? You obviously cleaned up somewhere." The dance music soared and faded, catching their attention.

Simon shook his head. "I was here of course – arrived last night. Didn't want to bother Kathy. Anyway, she's rejected me, so my handsome charms didn't work."

"Did you really want them to?"

He thought for a moment, then shrugged. "What I want doesn't matter. Kathy always gets what she wants."

*

The last waltz played at 3:00 in the morning. It was another hour before the house was finally quiet. Rory escorted Elly to her room, loosened his tie, and hoped she would loosen her clothing. Almost too tired to move, she sat on the edge of her bed and closed her eyes. He sat beside her and gently pressed his lips against hers. Her eyes flashed open. He quickly slipped both his arms around her corseted waist and

122

covered her face with light kisses. Pleased by the sensations, she smiled and allowed him to move down her cheek and neck. When he reached her exposed cleavage, she sped across the room.

He silently cursed himself. "Well… Good night." He stormed out the door.

Around the corner and down a long, dimly lit corridor, Isabelle spoke with a servant. She turned sharply, "Mr. Cook."

He stopped dead, red-faced, and panting.

She smiled at the servant and kept an eye on Rory. "Thank you, James. Get some sleep."

"Good night, Lady Richfield." He bowed and left.

Rory and Isabelle were alone. "You seem out of sorts, Mr. Cook."

"No, ma'am, it's just very late. Thank you for a most wonderful evening. Good night."

"It appears the evening didn't end so wonderfully."

"Good night." He bowed and walked away.

"Rory."

He stopped again, took a breath, and turned around.

She spoke quietly. "You were with Elly. What happened?"

His breath came hard and fast. "It's very late."

"What - happened?"

"Nothing."

A smile slowly spread across her beautiful face. "I - am - so - sorry."

Rory's blood raged. The blue of her eyes was the same blue as the gaslights and he wanted to smash them all. She opened the door to her boudoir and went inside. He stood in the hall, watching her take down her hair. It fell in impossibly heavy cascades of chestnut, thick and luxurious. She shook it over her naked shoulders and turned to face him. Standing perfectly still, smiling slightly, she drew him in like a magnet. His better judgment told him to run. His worse judgment won out. He went inside and closed the door behind him.

Chapter 14

Friday, December 25, 1903

"Happy Christmas, Daddy!"

"Hmm? What?" Not sure where he was, head aching from a night of rich food and too much champagne, Jeremy woke from a troubled sleep and rubbed his crusty eyes. Evan stood by the bed. "Oh, Happy Christmas, Evan."

Evan bounced into bed, snuggled under the covers, and hugged him hard.

"So, was Father Christmas good to you?"

"You and Mummy were good to me."

"Whatever do you think we had to do with it?"

"Oh, come now, Daddy. I'm not still a baby, believing in Father Christmas."

Jeremy stroked the boy's fine blond hair. "No, you're not a baby anymore. More's the pity. You were a very nice baby."

He sat up demanding, "What am I now then?"

Jeremy laughed. "You are a most engaging little boy. All too soon you will be a young man and I will be an old man. Don't blame your father for wanting you to stay little as long as possible."

"You'll never be old."

"Who do you think I am then, Merlin? Do you think I youthen, rather than growing old, like everyone else?"

"I don't want you to grow old."

"Well, darling boy, that makes two of us. Just stay with me. Keep me young."

Evan stared up with a creased forehead. "Of course I'll stay with you. Where would I go?"

Jeremy put a teasing finger on Evan's nose. Evan looked at it with crossed eyes and Jeremy scolded, "Don't do that!" They laughed and held each other tight.

Evan yawned. "Mummy's with Uncle Simon. I didn't know he was coming for Christmas."

"None of us knew. It was a surprise."

"I like surprises."

"Hmm."

"Don't you?"

"Not always."

"Are you angry he's here?"

He was furious, but didn't want to show it. "No, certainly not angry. Just... curious."

"Don't you like Uncle Simon anymore?"

"Of course I like him. He is one of my oldest friends."

"Are you angry he's with Mummy?"

He hesitated. "I am not pleased."

"But you like all Mummy's friends."

"Do I?"

"Don't you?"

"Why so many questions?" Frantic to stop his chatter, Jeremy tickled him and pushed him out of bed. "Come along, assistant chef. Let's see how Max is doing with our goose."

Three hours later, Jeremy, Katherine, Evan, Max, and the uninvited guest Simon Camden were enjoying a very merry Christmas. A crackling fire and two-dozen candles made them forget that freezing rain pelted the windows. Jeremy's goose was a masterpiece. He carved, Max served, and everyone ate. The diamond ring felt heavy in Jeremy's pocket. How was he going to give it to Katherine with Simon in the room?

Simon talked nonstop about his American tour. "It was revolting. I'm posed in my most poetic attitude. Juliet says, '*Ay me!*' I say, '*She speaks: O, speak again, bright angel!*' And I'm answered by a mule. A mule! *HEE-HAW, HEE-HAW*. Worst of all, no one in the audience seemed to notice."

"You're lucky." Katherine's mouth was full of a drumstick. "If they had, they might have noticed that a forty year old man was trying to play seventeen."

Simon pretended to be insulted. "How dare you! I'm a great actor. I can play anything." He tossed his head and threw a bun at her.

The bun bounced off her shoulder into her lap. "The critics agreed with me." She threw it back and he caught it mid-air.

"London critics, Kathy." He looked down his nose. "In Ohio, I was a star."

She burst out laughing. "Jerry, can you stand the ego?"

Jeremy smiled slightly. "Your Romeo was brilliant, Simon. The critics were very wrong."

"There, you see!" He gleefully pointed to Jeremy. "Here's a man with taste." Max started to remove a plate of bones and Simon grabbed his arm. "How about you, Max, did you like my Romeo?"

Max smiled shyly. "Oh, I did, sir, very much... only..." he leaned to one side, balancing on one foot.

"Only what?"

"Well, sir..." his brow wrinkled. "The young lady, sir..."

"Yes, what about her, didn't you like her?"

"Oh yes, sir, she was lovely, just a bit..." he swayed center, landing on two feet, "...young, I thought sir."

Katherine doubled over with laughter. "Oh, Max, thank you. Thank you!" She laughed until tears ran down her cheeks.

Max turned red and Jeremy said, "Leave the dishes, Max. Sit down and eat something. It's Christmas."

Max smiled. "Oh, thank you, sir." He pulled a chair next to Evan and helped himself from the ample platters of food.

Simon smiled lovingly. "It should have been you, Kathy."

"Oh, right!" She caught her breath and wiped her eyes. "There's nothing worse than middle-aged actors playing Romeo and Juliet. The critics would have had a party."

"I don't mean in London, you twit."

"Where then, in Ohio, with the mules?" She started laughing again.

Simon enjoyed her teasing. "Yes, and in New York, and Boston, and Washington, and Atlanta. They're marvelous cities full of fascinating people. I met Sam Smelling in New York."

Katherine made a face. "That newspaper chap, with the nose?"

"Oh, Kathy, you'd still make an enchanting Juliet."

Katherine shook her head. "Oh please, Simon. Offer me Lady Capulet, and I'll jump for it."

Jeremy raised an eyebrow. "You'd jump?"

Simon beamed. "What about Gertrude?"

"Yes, please!"

"To my Claudius."

She sat up, excited. "Yes!"

"It's yours." He pointed a finger. "Next winter in Delhi."

She lurched back. "Delhi, in India?"

Evan chirped, "Is there a part for me?"

Absolutely horrified, Jeremy lurched from his chair and carried an empty platter to the kitchen. A moment later, Katherine followed. Jeremy felt weak and tired as he leaned both hands on the cold porcelain sink. When she asked what was wrong, he shook his head, closed his eyes, and said nothing. She quietly demanded, "Please Jerry, you've been acting strange all day. What's happened?" He stared at the dirty platter, and she whispered, "You're frightening me."

Tears filled his eyes. "I'm frightening you?"

"Dear God." She took his hand, led him from the kitchen into his dark bedroom, and closed the door. The fire had not been lit. She shivered and turned up a lamp. Jeremy stood by the window, staring vacantly at rain beating against the glass. She joined him and he put his arms around her. He kissed her forehead and felt their hearts beating almost in time.

He sighed wearily. "Do you have any idea how much I love you?" She squeezed him tighter. "You are the most precious thing in my life. You know that, don't you? You and…" he hesitated, "…our son." His throat tightened. Tears blurred his sight. Afraid he would start weeping uncontrollably; he pushed her away and crossed to the cold marble hearth. He rested a foot on the grate, and placed a finger over his lips. "I don't want to say something stupid. Something I'll regret for the rest of my life."

Shivering, Katherine sat on the upholstered love seat. "Whatever it is, just say it."

He blurted out, "Has Simon asked you to marry him?"

"Yes."

"What have you answered?" His limbs were tight as bow strings.

"I haven't answered, actually." She trilled a nervous laugh. "Can you believe it? After all these years he still wants to make me an honest woman." She shrugged her shoulders. "I don't understand him at all.

He's at the height of his career, rich, handsome, still young enough to catch any beautiful heiress in the land, and he wants me."

"Of course he wants you." Jeremy tried to stay calm, but his voice rose with each line. "You are the most generous, tolerant, nurturing woman in England. You are also beautiful, a brilliant actress, and you deserve someone a damn sight better than Simon - Bloody - Camden!"

Thrown off guard, she straightened up. Her fingers toyed nervously with lace on her skirt. "I'm becoming less generous and tolerant by the moment."

Jeremy lightly pounded the marble. "It hasn't been easy, all these years, watching you waste your time with Eric, write endless letters to Simon, and then that pompous ass, Owen."

She glared. "But he was your..."

"I know, I know, I threw you together." His hands flew up in defense. "I am sorry. But all three men are hopelessly unfit, one way or the other."

She sprang to her feet. "And how fit are you then? Are you so much better?"

He shouted, "Of course I'm better. A hundred times better." Remembering Simon was nearby; he lowered his voice and sat next to her. "I will be here for you and Evan, every day for the rest of my life. We three need each other, on-stage-and-off. Can you even imagine sharing a life like ours, twenty-four-hours-a-day, with Simon?"

Startled, she stood and slowly backed away. "Jerry, do you really believe that you have been available twenty-four-hours-a-day? I love you more than anyone else in the world, but I've spent fifteen years watching you go to young men. I went to Eric because I couldn't go to you. I couldn't leave you either."

She turned her back and rubbed her head, breathing hard. "You're not to blame. I've had plenty of opportunities to marry, if I'd really wanted to. You didn't make me stay... Well, you did in a way -- You're wonderful. You're brilliant. My happiest hours are watching you *on-stage*, and being with you *on-stage*.

"When we're alone," she smiled, "you understand me totally. You're loving, accepting, full of humor, no matter what horror I invite upon myself. You're always there when I need you." He reached out his hand, but she stayed where she was. "Well, you're almost always there."

"I will be from now on, I promise. I'll take down those doors between the floors and never invite another man into this house. I want our life to stay as it is. For God's sake, Katie, please, marry *me*!"

"Now you're raving like King Lear." She started toward the door, shaking her head. He stepped in front of her, took both her hands, and went down on one knee. She lowered her eyes. "Dear God, no."

He gazed up adoringly. "You and the boy are my whole life. Everything I am, everything I ever hope to do or be, depends on you. You are my support, my strength, and my only true love. '*Not from the stars do I my judgment pluck; And yet methinks I have astronomy,*'"

She tried to pull away. "Stop it, Jerry. This is absurd."

"'*But not to tell of good or evil luck, Of plagues, of dearths, or seasons' quality;*'"

She jerked her hands, trying to free them.

He held them tighter and inched closer so that his knee touched her leg. "'*Nor can I fortune to brief minutes tell, Pointing to each his thunder, rain and wind,*'"

"Will you stop this!"

"'*Or say with princes if it shall go well, By oft predict that I in heaven find.*'" He gripped her hands, and stayed perfectly still, until she looked at him. His voice was a velvet whisper. "'*But from thine eyes my knowledge I derive, And, constant stars, in them I read such art As truth and beauty shall together thrive, If from thyself to store thou wouldst convert;*'"

Tears filled her eyes, and she tossed her head.

"'*Or else of thee, thus I prognosticate: Thy end is truth's, and beauty's doom the date.*'" He stood, took her in his arms, and kissed her with all the passion he possessed. They held each other for a long time.

When they finally relaxed, she stepped away, wiping her eyes. "That was a great scene, Jerry." Her voice cracked, "That was brilliant."

"That wasn't acting. Can't you tell the difference?"

He reached for her again, but she pulled away, shivering. "I'm cold, let's go back." She was out the door before he remembered the ring in his pocket. He followed her back to the dining room.

The fire roared, fresh candles burned gaily, and Max had set the table for pudding. The sudden brightness stung their eyes. Simon and Evan were on the floor, making tin soldiers fall from a toy hot-air-balloon.

When Simon looked up at Jeremy, his playful smile dropped. "Who died? Or was it something I said? Am I being evicted?" He stood up.

Evan watched, but stayed with his toys.

Katherine put her arms around Jeremy's waist. "Jerry's terrified that I'm going to marry you and leave him."

Evan's mouth dropped open and he sat up.

Simon panicked. "Looking at you now, I'm terrified that you won't."

She smiled. "Don't exaggerate, Simon, you're not terrified."

"You don't know how I feel." His chest rose and fell with quick breaths.

She sat in her chair at the table. "I don't know. I'm sorry."

"That wasn't a flippant proposal, Kathy." He sat next to her, gently held her shoulders, and looked into her eyes. "I agonized over it for a year. You really have been all over the world, in my mind."

She stroked his manicured beard. "I believe you, darling. I never thought it was flippant." He kissed the palm of her hand.

Jeremy sat in his chair. The two men studied each other. Jeremy leaned back, closed his eyes, and sighed deeply. "I've been dreading this moment for fifteen years. I never thought it would be you."

Simon comically twisted his neck and looked over both shoulders. "Who were you expecting then, Henry Irving?" They all laughed.

Max appeared from the kitchen. "If everyone's back, perhaps it's time for pudding."

"And Christmas crackers." Evan jumped from the floor and ran to the basket of paper cylinders. With an excited smile, he chose a bright blue one, offered his mother one end, and firmly gripped the other. They both pulled and laughed as it went off with a loud, BANG!

The doorbell rang and Max tottered from the kitchen. "Can't imagine who that is. We've already had Father Christmas."

A moment later, Eric Bates swept into the room. His face was flushed and his hands were shaking. Speaking quickly, his voice sounded high and strained. His sentences ran together. "Sorry to bother you lot, but..." He stopped, surprised. "Oh, hello Simon... Jerry, Kathy... we've got a disaster on our hands." Katherine joined him on the sofa. He sat, shivering. Everyone else was silent, waiting for him to continue. "Two Scotland Yard officers just paid me a visit. On Christmas night. We have a houseful. Hilda's fit to be tied.

"A few hours ago, Peg McCarthy burned down Mrs. Potter's boarding house. Mrs. Potter jumped out a window and died hitting the pavement. Two elderly ladies were there. They're unharmed, just homeless. Apparently all the actors were away." He stopped for breath. "Then, early this morning, Tommy Quinn had a murder in his brothel: the seventeen-year-old nephew of a Duchess. Peg and Tommy seem to have run off together."

The blood drained from Jeremy's face. "Holy Mother of God! What were they doing together?"

"Apparently she serviced his customers." Eric shuddered. "God knows what she did for them. Nothing conventional, I'm sure."

"Where are they now?"

He shrugged. "No one knows. I was hoping you might."

"Bloody hell!" Suddenly sweating, Jeremy wiped his brow. "I hope Tommy stays clear of me. On second thought, if he did come to me, I'd give him money enough to get to the continent."

Simon snorted, "You can't save him this time, Jerry. This won't be a few months in Reading Gaol. If he's involved in a murder, it'll be the gallows."

"Dear God in heaven." Jeremy put a hand over his mouth.

Katherine was shaking. "I can't believe it. Peg was always wildly eccentric, but a torch in Elly's face, and now arson, and…"

Jeremy snorted a laugh. "For years I've been trying to get Hilda to move the apprentices into a decent boardinghouse. Now she'll have to." He stared at the floor. "I'm still trying to fathom Tommy with Peg. What a horrible waste. They're such great talents."

Simon gasped, "'Great talents'? They're murderers, Jerry."

He held up his hands. "No, they are not. They are foolish and reckless and they pick the wrong friends. Damn! Perhaps they do belong together. Was anyone else involved?"

Eric stood up. "Archibald Perry was at Tommy's, with a houseful of other men. They've all been arrested. I didn't recognize the other names. Sorry you lot, but we've got a houseful. I've got to get back. I wouldn't have had to come over, if you owned a bloody telephone." Now he was shouting.

Jeremy glared at him. "I will not give up my privacy and allow one of those repulsive contraptions into my house."

"Oh, never mind. Bye all. Oh and, yes, um… Happy Christmas." He started for the door then swung back. "Oh, I've notified Peg's cover for the Second Witch, but I don't have anyone for *The Magistrate* to cover Beatie. None of our women can pass for sixteen. Can Elly Fielding do it? I know she's not ready, but better her than Eddy in a wig."

Jeremy raised an eyebrow. "No, she cannot do it, not yet. But, as you say, better her than Eddy in a wig. I shall coach her myself." He paced aimlessly, his mind filled with terrifying images of Tommy and Peg swinging on the gallows.

Eric nodded. "Thanks, Jerry. See you lot tomorrow." Max held the door as he hurried out.

Simon looked at Jeremy. "Since when does an actor-manager coach understudies?"

Jeremy snapped back, "She is absolutely green and has not had the chance to learn bad habits. If I coach her now, it may save me a lot of grief later. Besides, it will give me something to do. This lack of employment is driving me mad."

Katherine laughed sadly. "Can you believe that, Simon? He considers eight performances a week a lack of employment. God forbid the man should have a leisure hour in the day. So Jerry, that means you've finished staging *The Tempest* on paper?"

"Yes. The joy is over and the drudgery begins." He stared into the fire.

Simon raised an eyebrow. "What's he on about?"

Katherine sighed. "Jerry's imagination is his playground. Perfect imaginary actors give perfect imaginary performances. Unfortunately, he expects human actors to be clairvoyant, immediately reproducing what is in his mind. When we can't do it, he rages into black moods and we all suffer."

Simon curled his lip. "Sound's charming. Remind me never to work for him."

Jeremy sneered, "Please excuse me." He started toward his room and Evan chased after him. He hugged the boy long and hard. "It's all right, Evan. I am not going anywhere. And neither are you." He glared at Katherine and Simon, and took to his bed.

Chapter 15

Saturday, December 26, 1903

The day after Christmas, the apprentices moved into a very pleasant boardinghouse. There was no matinee, so Elly Fielding left her few belongings, hurried to the theatre, and spent three hideous hours mending costume tears. Finally released, she carried all the costumes downstairs. It took twelve trips. When she dragged the last few as far as stage level, she collapsed on the stairs. They felt heavy as lead, piled across her lap. She leaned back and closed her eyes.

"MISS FIELDING!"

Waking from a deep sleep, she jumped up and spilled four expensive garments onto the feet of Eric Bates. "I'm sorry sir!" She was grateful when a man behind Eric helped pile them into her arms. She stared into the laughing blue eyes of American journalist Sam Smelling.

"Hi, Elly."

She smiled back. "Hello, Sam."

Knowing how ridiculous she looked, she waddled into the quick change dressing-room and hung up the clothes. That evening's *Macbeth* was sold out. She knew she would never get a seat, and went into the house expecting to stand with the ushers. When she saw Simon Camden and Sam Smelling in Eric Bates's box, they waved her up, and moved apart, so an empty chair sat between them. They were dressed in beautiful evening clothes. She wore a soiled school frock, so smiled back, pulled at the wrinkled shoulders, and shook her head. Simon gestured grandly, demanding that she join them. As the house went to black, she made a dash up the stairs and into the box. As the stage lights came up, she squeezed between the two men, glanced into Sam's laughing eyes, and felt a giggle inside.

Thunder crashed, lightning lit up the scene, and she turned to see Simon spellbound. Throughout the entire act, his eyes were glued to the stage. When Lady Macbeth entered, he beamed with love and pride.

The First Act curtain fell and Simon stared at the dark footlights. Sam and Elly glanced at each other, waiting for Simon to speak.

Finally, he sat back, scowling. "This is incredible. This production should be seen all over the world. It's all-well-and-good for a limited London run to be sold out, but this is remarkable." He stroked his chin. "Those two are extraordinary -- as good as any pair in the English speaking theatre. Damn!" He slapped his thigh. "The whole production's absolutely fantastic. Jerry's a genius. They say he's a bastard to work for. So be it. If that's what it takes, I applaud him."

Elly stared at Simon's steely-gray eyes and glistening silvery-blond hair. He seemed powerful as a lion, and she longed to stroke his long silky mane.

His eyes narrowed. "Sam, I know you love uncovering crimes of passion, but you write damn good commentary as well. Somehow the whole world must be told about this production. How can we make that happen?"

"I've got some ideas, actually… but first, let's find out what Eric Bates plans to do with it."

Simon blew in the air. "He's provincial. He's no plans at all. He's ready to let this close and be lost forever." He pounded his fist into the palm of his hand, shouting, "I won't let that happen." Elly lurched back and Simon chuckled. "I'm sorry. Did I frighten you?" Very gently, he ran the back of his fingers over her cheek, around her chin, down her smooth throat, and under her collar. Her eyes closed with pleasure and Simon chuckled. "Look at her blush. I love this girl." When Sam lightly shook his head, Simon removed his hand, stood and stretched. "I'm parched, let's find the bar."

Chapter 16

Sunday, December 27, 1903

Jeremy O'Connell found a copy of the *Daily Mail* on his dressing table. It was folded open to an article titled, *A London Christmas Eve*. A cartoon of a nose was next to the by-line, "by Sam Smell, 'The Man With The Nose For News.'" He picked up the paper and was quickly laughing out loud. Sam's description made him see Isabelle's ball all over again. Sam poked fun at everyone, without being unkind to anyone. The only person he ridiculed was himself, an American bumpkin among upper-crust British society.

Jeremy turned the page over, continued reading down the column, and caught sight of the art gallery notices. One read:

Premier Exhibition:
ROBERT DENNISON
Oils and Pastels
Gildstein Gallery
January 5th - 10th

This was the very Robert Dennison responsible for Elly Fielding's flight to London. Whether Dennison had done her a service or a disservice, he was a school-master who had seduced a student.

Jeremy was startled from his daydreaming when Eddy Edwards told him Michael Burns was out sick, and understudy Rory Cook could finally play the role he had covered for a year. Jeremy was sorry about Michael, but thrilled for Rory.

As he expected, Rory's performance was wonderful. At the final curtain call, the company of sixteen actors joined hands, bowing together. Jeremy turned and acknowledged Rory. Grinning from ear-to-ear, Rory stepped forward, raised both arms, and took a grand solo bow. The audience, other actors, and backstage crew screamed and applauded.

Rory rejoined the line. The actors bowed together, as the stage curtain swooshed heavily to the ground.

Immediately, Rory was smothered with kisses and congratulations. Jeremy hugged him like the proudest of fathers. Rory found Elly in the crowd, swung her around and kissed her. "I was so afraid you wouldn't be here. Then I saw you and Sam, up in the box." He kissed her again then pushed her away. "I'm sorry! I'm getting makeup on your frock."

Elly laughed happily. "I don't care a bit."

"Well, I do. I'll change and see you at the 'Lion." He sped off stage and up the stairs.

In a flurry of capes and scarves, wig-master Eugene pranced across the stage, spotted Elly, put his hands on his hips, and stamped his foot. "There you are!" He reached inside his voluminous drapes, pulled out a letter, and presented it with a flourish.

She looked at the handwriting and gasped, "Thanks so much. I'm sorry I caused you trouble."

"Girls always cause trouble." He flounced away.

She raced after him. "Is Michael all right?"

He kept walking. "Runny nose and sneezing. He'll be right as rain come Tuesday. T'ra, darling!" He waved his hand and left the theatre.

*

Jeremy was nearly dressed when Elly appeared at his dressing-room door. "Miss Fielding. Our boy did well, today."

"Yes, sir. I've never been so proud."

He smiled at Elly's reflection while combing his hair. "To what do I owe this pleasure?"

She handed him her letter. "Eugene brought this from Michael."

He took the envelope and read:

Dear Michael,

I cannot believe I will be in London in only nine days. I have seen the gallery notices with my name. It all feels like a dream. Mother has changed her holiday so I will be able to stay the full week, as originally planned. I so look forward to meeting Sandra, and letting you two show me the town.

Do you remember my telling you about a runaway student? Her father telegraphed that she has gotten herself all the way to Paris. How's that for pluck? Yours,

Rob

Jeremy tilted his head. "Well done. May I keep this?"

"Please."

He put the letter in his pocket and crossed his arms. "So, Isabelle's younger brother has bought you a bit of time, and it seems that Isabelle has some news."

"I know. She asked me to tea tomorrow."

He closed his eyes and shuddered. "We are all going to tea tomorrow."

She smiled at his clowning. "May I speak freely, sir?"

"Of course."

She gazed up with moist green eyes. "I have been very happy since coming to London."

"Really? A lot of dreadful things have happened to you."

"Many more lovely ones." She shrugged her shoulders. "Ever since I was fourteen," she looked down at her hands, "since I learned I was betrothed to Sir John Garingham, I looked upon my eighteenth birthday as the day of my death -- the end of any possible happiness." When she looked up again, her face was glowing. "I have already had eleven extra days. Eleven miraculous days I never thought I could have." Jeremy looked horrified, and she stuttered, "D'Do I sound like a lunatic?"

"No, not at all." He wanted to reassure her, but could not think how.

Embarrassed, she looked down and stayed silent. When she looked up again, she was blinking back tears. "I just want you to know, sir, that you are the first mature gentleman who has ever treated me with kindness and respect, and whatever happens to me, I will always be grateful."

"Thank you." His inflection was flat. He leaned his elbows on his knees. "Now tell me what has happened. Why are you suddenly afraid?"

Her voice was a tearful whisper. "Robert Dennison's best painting, at least the one he believes to be his best, is titled *Autumn Lady*." She swallowed. "It is a portrait of Elisa Roundtree."

"Is it a true likeness?"

"It is quite perfect." She hugged herself. "It is a most beautiful portrait."

"Painted by a man in love with his model?"

She shrugged her shoulders.

"Elly Fielding has not yet been on-stage. Few people know her, and she has powerful friends to protect her."

"A hundred people saw her at Lord Richfield's Christmas party. It only takes one to see the portrait and ask a question."

"There must be fifty galleries in London, each giving twenty shows a year. While not impossible, the likelihood of someone recognizing Elisa Roundtree is slight. Anyone who might would probably think the likeness a coincidence." He gazed at the ceiling. "Obviously you have not asked Dennison to withdraw *Autumn Lady* from the exhibit."

She shook her head.

"Would he withdraw it, if he thought it might do you harm?"

"I am sure he would, and in doing so, lessen his chances of success. I know little about art, but I do know that a single painting has made an artist's career. He has worked very hard and very long. I won't jeopardize his future."

Jeremy nodded, pursing his lips. "Now, *that* sounds lunatic… as love is always lunatic." He smiled fondly. "I am moved by your stolen days, but you must not believe that they are stolen. Those days belong to you. We only ever have *today*, and every happy day is a gift." He looked toward the door. "Come in, Mr. Smelling. We are waxing philosophical."

Sam Smelling stood in the doorway, holding Elly's coat. His eyes were full of concern. "I didn't mean to eavesdrop, but that was great." He pulled up a chair, and pushed the hair from his eyes. "Waxing philosophical is one of my favourite things. I thought the young lady might want her coat." He handed it to her.

Jeremy pointed. "Sam! I didn't thank you for that brilliant bit in your article. I absolutely adore being compared to a quill pen. What was it you wrote, 'consummate physical grace, elegant articulation, with a dangerously scratchy edge'?"

Sam laughed. "Something like that." He looked at Elly. "Who's Elisa Roundtree?"

She turned away, putting her hand over her mouth.

"Whoever she is, and whatever trouble she's in, I can probably help. I'd like to, if I can."

Elly looked startled, but Jeremy was pleased. "Yes, Sam. You probably can help us. Are you free for tea with Lady Richfield tomorrow?"

"Absolutely."

Chapter 17

Monday, December 28, 1903

At 3:00 the next afternoon, attacked by stinging needles of frozen rain, Elly, Rory, and Jeremy stepped from a hansom cab and scurried inside Isabelle's mansion. Isabelle, Katherine, and Sam were already in the drawing room, talking with two gentlemen in somber suits. Isabelle introduced her solicitor, Roger Foxhall, and Foxhall's junior, James MacCain. A steaming bowl of mulled wine sat near the roaring fireplace. A footman poured dark-red liquid into heavy cut-glass goblets.

They sipped sweet wine and Isabelle spoke to the sofa. "Evan, darling, Lucy is so looking forward to seeing you. Why don't you go up to the nursery and surprise her?"

Reluctantly, Even left his hiding place and scurried upstairs.

Isabelle invited everyone to sit down. The room was warm, but Elly shivered. Isabelle took her hand and they both sat on a sofa. Solicitor Foxhall and his junior sat in straight-back chairs and spread papers over a low table in front of them. Jeremy, Katherine, Rory, and Sam made themselves comfortable in chairs and sofas.

After sipping his mulled wine, Foxhall curled his handlebar mustache and began. "Upon the request of Lady Richfield, I sent my junior, Mr. MacCain, to discover what he could about the parentage and possible assets of Miss Elisa Roundtree. Mr. MacCain first checked the General Register Office, Somerset House in London. Finding the documents to be confused, he went to Settle, Miss Fielding's home village in Yorkshire, to check other copies of the same documents. I gave Mr. MacCain instructions not to disturb the town residents."

After a moment's silence, Sam asked, "So, Mr. MacCain got nothing?"

Foxhall looked down his nose. "No, sir, certainly not nothing. Just, not quite as much as we hoped. I will let Mr. MacCain explain."

The young solicitor looked very nervous. He straightened his starched collar, adjusted his silver-rimmed spectacles, and looked around the room as if presenting an academic address. "Lady Richfield, Mr. Foxhall,

Miss Roundtree, ladies and gentlemen." He smiled, pausing for effect. Everyone waited. "Unfortunately, the local town records in Miss Roundtree's home village of Settle are in exactly the same disarray as the ones in the London Registry Office. I was unable to discover any information that I can call credible."

Sam leaned into MacCain. "In what way were they in 'disarray'?"

"Well sir, they are all copies, of course, the original documents being in the possession of the persons involved, and village clerks may not always be careful in their work." MacCain picked up a paper. "For instance, the birth certificate of Elisa Roundtree is dated December 23, 1885, and the time stated as 2:15 p.m."

Sam looked at Elly and she shrugged her shoulders.

MacCain checked his paper. "The mother was Bertha Roundtree, formally VonLeichter."

Trying to hide her excitement, Isabelle clutched Elly's hand. "VonLeichter was my aunt's married name. Bertha could have been her daughter."

Elly flushed as MacCain continued. "And the father was Charles Roundtree."

"*Charles* Roundtree?" Elly stared in surprise.

Sam narrowed his eyes. "Who's Charles Roundtree?"

"My uncle, he died before I was born."

"How long before you were born?"

"I have no idea. No, wait." She concentrated. "I don't know exactly, but he was working on the Suez Canal. He was an engineer. There was an accident and he was killed. My Aunt Lillian talks about him when father isn't around. Father hates stories about his brother Charles."

Sam was on the edge of his seat. "What's your father's first name?"

"Anthony. Charles was the elder brother, there's a family portrait…"

Sam leaned into her, listening hard.

Her brows drew together as she concentrated. "There's a painting in Aunt Lillian's room."

Jeremy prompted, "Lillian is your father's unmarried sister?"

"Yes, they were the three oldest children: Charles, Lillian, and Anthony. There were two younger children who died when they were still little. After their mother died, Aunt Lillian took over running the household."

Sam turned to Jeremy. "Jerry, you're the historian. What do you know about the Suez Canal?"

Jeremy concentrated, his elbows on his knees. "Well, Elly was born at the end of 1885," he put a finger over his lips. "As far as I remember, by 1885 the British owned shares of the canal, but had given up all other claims. The work was mainly done by French engineers," he pointed a finger, "...and German. If Charles Roundtree's wife was German, it is possible he was employed by her family's firm. I remember the papers were full of stories about fortunes being instantly made and lost, engineering firms pouring into the area, competing for contracts, practically killing each other for profit. And reports of terrible casualties from fever and building accidents."

Sam turned back to the solicitor. "Mr. MacCain, who signed Miss Roundtree's birth certificate?"

MacCain read from his paper. "Dr. Frederick Vickers."

"Was there anything else on that document?"

"No sir."

"Was there a death certificate for Charles Roundtree?"

"In London, sir. None in Settle."

"What was the date?"

"Well sir, here is where the records get muddled." After adjusting his spectacles, he sat up with a self-important air. "The recorded death of Charles Roundtree is December 26, 1885."

"Where?"

"In Suez, Egypt."

"What's wrong with that?"

"Well sir, there was no marriage license for Charles Roundtree and Bertha VonLeichter at either office."

Isabelle shrugged, "Her mother was German. They could have been married anywhere."

MacCain continued, "Much to my surprise, I did find a marriage license for Anthony Roundtree and Bertha Roundtree."

Sam lurched forward. "Bertha Roundtree? Are you sure? Not Bertha VonLeichter?"

Jeremy was intrigued. "If Charles Roundtree had married Bertha VonLeichter *before* his brother married her, her name would have appeared as Bertha Roundtree on that marriage certificate."

MacCain nodded, "Well sir, it is most curious. The names were certainly Anthony Roundtree and Bertha Roundtree."

Sam asked, "Who performed the ceremony?"

"Reverend Laurence Folen."

"Who witnessed it?"

"Elizabeth Graves."

"What was the date?"

"Well sir… December 23, 1885 at 2:10 p.m."

Isabelle sat up. "A wedding, three days *before* the woman's first husband died?"

"Yes, Lady Richfield. That is the disarray I am talking about. I checked the death certificate of Bertha Roundtree and it is also dated December 23, 1885, the day of Miss Roundtree's birth."

Jeremy threw up his hands. "We all know that Elly's -- that is -- Elisa's mother died in childbirth."

"Yes sir, but it is the time of death, sir."

"What about it?"

"The time of death is 2:13 p.m., and the time of Miss Roundtree's birth is 2:14 p.m., so you see, these times must be incorrect."

Katherine let out a gasp. "Oh, that poor woman!" Her hand went over her mouth,

Sam turned to her. "Is it possible for a child to be born after the mother's dead?"

"Yes," Katherine was practically in tears, "if they can cut it out fast enough." Standing up and crossing her arms, she turned her back and stared out a window.

A shocked silence fell over the room. MacCain blushed. His voice shook. "Well then, it is possible that the certificate is correct."

Sam narrowed his eyes. "Who signed the death certificate?"

MacCain checked his notes. "Dr. Frederick Vickers and Reverend Laurence Folen."

Foxhall pursed his lips. "Perhaps they called a priest to administer the last rites."

"I remember Father Folen." Elly sat up, putting a hand on her forehead. "When I was little. He was always nice to me. He gave me sweets… and ices in the summer." She smiled, enjoying the memory. "I remember one very strict governess… Father Folen held me back after services, and took me to the rectory to tell me funny stories. The governess hated it, but she couldn't say, 'no,' to the vicar." Deflated after her happy recollection, she sat back.

Sam asked, "What happened to him?"

She shook her head. "I just remember one Sunday he wasn't there anymore, and the new priest treated me like all the other children."

"Father Folen treated you better than the other children?"

"Yes."

"Do you know why?"

She shook her head. "I just thought he liked me."

Jeremy peered at the papers on the table. "Is the wedding recorded in the local church registry?"

MacCain checked his notes. "Yes sir, but the signatures of Anthony Roundtree and Bertha Roundtree are both written in the same hand. The date is December 23rd, but the time is blank.

Katherine hugged herself. "This is intolerable." Everyone stared at her. Isabelle lowered her face, covering her eyes. The tension in the room was electric. Katherine glared. "You *men* have no idea, have you?" They guiltily glanced at one another.

Only Rory, the youngest among them, dared to speak the horror they all imagined. His voice was a monotone. "It appears that Anthony Roundtree assumed his brother was dead, and married his brother's widow to gain custody of his niece. The Von in front of the name tells us that Elly's mother was well-born. If the VonLeichter family was involved in building the Suez Canal, they might have made a great deal of money, which belongs to the heiress."

He looked at Elly and she stared back with huge eyes. "It is possible that Anthony Roundtree married Bertha so he could protect her unborn child, but noting the kind of father he has been, it seems more likely that he simply wanted to claim her inheritance."

Isabelle looked up in dismay. "Then why is he so eager to marry her off? He'll lose the estate to her husband. Why not just keep her locked up at home and keep her money?"

Appalled by the idea, Elly caught her breath.

Jeremy spoke softly. "Elly, you were betrothed as a child."

"Yes sir."

"You told me the man's name, I have forgotten it."

"Sir John Garingham."

"Have you any idea what hold Sir John has over your father?"

"No sir."

Sam sat back, sighed loudly, and crossed his legs. "It must be a good one for Roundtree to give up the golden goose."

The silly reference broke the tension and they were all grateful for a laugh.

Rory drummed his fingers. "We need to verify the date of Charles Roundtree's death. If men working on the canal were dying at the rate Mr. O'Connell remembers, it may not be easy. If the date is correct, considering the change in time zones, and if the marriage was illegal, the court would have free rein to assign an alternate guardianship for Elly until she reaches the age of twenty-one. Then she can take control of her estate; the amount, and location of which we also need to discover. Even if there is no estate, an alternate guardianship would protect her from this questionable marriage. If the date is incorrect, and Charles Roundtree died before two o'clock in the afternoon on December the 23rd, Greenwich Mean Time, the marriage could be legal... Even so..." He looked at Katherine. "Miss Stewart, am I correct in assuming that you believe no woman in the latter stages of childbirth is lucid enough to enter into a bond of holy matrimony with her whole heart?"

"You're assumption is correct."

"Lady Richfield?"

Isabelle looked up. "I agree."

"Do you also agree that any legal contract signed by a woman in the latter stages of childbirth could be considered to be made under duress?"

"Absolutely!"

He looked at the solicitor. "Mr. Foxhall."

Foxhall turned to Rory. "Yes, Mr..."

"Cook."

"Mr. Cook."

"I believe Parliament is still debating the Wife's Sister's Bill, and a man is still prevented by law from marrying his deceased wife's sister."

"That is correct, Mr. Cook. Unfortunately for our case, it is legal for a woman to marry her deceased husband's brother." Foxhall brightly twirled his mustache. "Young man, you speak like a solicitor."

Rory smiled weakly. Had he stayed at Oxford, he might be working long hours in a cramped office, with dreary men like these two.

MacCain adjusted his silver-rimmed spectacles. "Ladies and gentlemen, there is just one more curiosity. I could not find Mrs. Roundtree's gravestone." He turned to Elly. "Miss Roundtree, do you know where your mother is buried?"

"No sir."

Sam raised his hand. "Mr. MacCain, who did you say witnessed the marriage license?"

He checked the paper again. "Elizabeth Graves."

Sam turned to Elly. "Do you know her?"

"No, but there's a large Graves family in town. Some of them work on the grounds."

Sam nodded. "This Elizabeth Graves is an old woman by now, if she's still alive. Do you know an old woman, maybe a Betty, or Beth, Lizzy, Eliza...?"

Elly thought, then shook her head. "No, I'm sorry."

"How about Dr. Vickers?"

She shook her head.

Isabelle turned to the young solicitor. "Have you anything more, Mr. MacCain?"

"No, ma'am."

She stood up and pulled the bell-cord. "I congratulate you, young man. You have done very well indeed. Ladies and gentlemen, it is time for some refreshment. I'm sure there will be further discussion, but that can be continued later." The butler Smythe appeared and she asked that tea be served immediately. As everyone stood and stretched, she extended her hand to the young solicitor. Blushing, MacCain adjusted his spectacles, took her hand, and made an awkward bow.

Rory, Sam, and Jeremy shared troubled looks. Sam asked Elly, "Tell me about Sir John Garingham."

She looked up in horror. "What do you want to know?"

"You like him that much?"

She giggled, but her laughter was dangerously close to tears.

Sam's brow creased as he brushed hair away from his forehead. "I'll find out what he's all about. I'll also find Father Laurence Folen, Dr.

Frederick Vickers, and Elizabeth Graves, or at least something about them."

Elly pleaded, "Will you really? Can you?" Fear radiated from her beautiful green eyes.

Sam spoke with absolute assurance. "I'm an investigator, Elly, 'The Man With The Nose For News.' This is what I do best. I can - and I will."

Chapter 18

Tuesday, December 29, 1903

Elly and Rory sat together at the back of the noisy rehearsal hall, full of actors. Rory begged, "Please Elly, do everything he says, even if it sounds lunatic. Just - do - it."

At exactly 1:00, Jeremy O'Connell entered. He spoke briefly about rehearsals for *The Tempest*, and took the scene list from Donald Moran. Elly had gone last in his previous class, so he called her first. Forcing her legs to move, she walked in front of the audience of actors, chose a spot on the back wall, and began.

> *"Gallop apace, you fiery-footed steeds,*
> *Towards Phoebus' lodging: Such a wagoner*
> *As Phaethon would whip you the west,*
> *And bring in cloudy night immediately…."*

Slowly relaxing, the words became fluid. A few more lines and, Jeremy's voice rang out.

"Stop!" His expression was hard, but calm. "You are speaking the lines simply and their sense is clear. That is good." He pointed a finger. "Now, let us see if we can find just the tiniest bit of Juliet to put with them, shall we?"

She whispered, "I want to. I don't know how."

"That is why I am here. Sit - down!"

Without taking her eyes off him, she pulled up a chair. The entire room was focused on Elly, but she was only aware of Jeremy O'Connell. He sat comfortably, leaning forward, legs apart, elbows resting on his knees, hands together. His piercing brown eyes seemed to bore through her. "What does Juliet want?"

"She wants the night to come and bring Romeo."

"Why?"

"She's in love with Romeo."

"What do you mean, 'she's in love'?"

She stared dumbly, praying for inspiration.

"What is it like to be in love?"

She bit her lip.

"What does it feel like?"

Frightened, she shook her head.

He waited for a few moments, then sat back and put a finger over his lips. He spoke quietly and distinctly. "What does it feel like to be in the arms of a man you care for?"

Imagining Robert's arms around her, she sat back and crossed her arms, hugging herself.

Jeremy smiled slightly. "At some time a man has touched you." He paused. "That simple touch has made you tremble."

Almost in a trance, she relived Simon Camden's finger brushing her throat. Her eyes blinked.

Jeremy nodded. "Good."

Her eyes went wide. *No*! *I can't be thinking of Simon Camden.*

"Don't banish him! Whoever he is, call him back. Hold on to him, you need his image."

His image was so bright it blinded: a silver lion's mane around fierce gray eyes. She shook her head, *This is wrong. Think of Robert.*

Jeremy shouted, "Bring him back. Damn it! Let him in!"

She obeyed. Simon's face glowed in her imagination.

Jeremy's eyes blazed. "You are surprised. You did not expect this particular man."

She shook her head, her eyes wide in disbelief.

"We cannot control our subconscious minds. Do not try. Just consider him a gift for Juliet. This is not real life, and I certainly do not suggest that you leave this room and act out your fantasies, but right now, this instant, he is your strongest image. Juliet needs him. Every actor has looked at a pretend love and pictured a true love. Now, close your eyes."

She obeyed.

"Do not answer out loud. What colour are his eyes?"

Oh, God, those powerful eyes.

"What colour is his hair? How is it cut, what is the texture?"

Her imagination was ahead of him. Her fingers were already deep in Simon's long silky hair. She stroked his silver beard.

"Feel the shape of his face."

Unaware that her body was gently shifting, she turned her face, imagining she was touching his.

"Feel his kiss."

A soft cry came from deep inside her.

From his seat in the audience, Rory stared, amazed and alarmed. The audience was riveted. Her emotions filled the room.

Jeremy leaned his elbows back down onto his knees. He whispered, "Look at me."

She tentatively opened her eyes. Totally vulnerable, she was ready to do anything he asked.

His eyes were strong and friendly. "Hello Juliet. You can see Romeo in your mind."

She nodded and a sort of sob bubbled from her throat.

He pointed to a spot on the wall above the audience. "There is the sun. Go and talk to it."

Elly stood up and effortlessly began, *"Gallop apace, you fiery-footed steeds,*

Towards Phoebus' lodging: …"

The audience listened, amazed at every word. Every nuance was real, alive and captivating.

When she said, *"…and Romeo*

Leap into these arms…" Simon Camden loomed before her, powerful, sensual, and sweet. On the closing, *"…and every tongue that speaks*

But Romeo's name speaks heavenly eloquence," she felt him stroke her neck. Her eyes squeezed shut and her body cramped.

The actors broke into applause. Barely aware of them, she looked tentatively at Jeremy.

"Good." He smiled and winked an eye.

Thrilled and relieved, she broke into a smile. Aching to embrace him, she lowered her eyes, quietly returning to her seat.

Nancy Cushman bellowed, "Mr. O'Connell, what have you done? The poor child will never be the same." The room exploded with laughter and a release of tension.

At 7:15, Elly finished carrying costumes downstairs. Her hair was tied back in a rag, and a light sweat shone on her pale skin. She delivered the last costumes to the quick change room, came out, and clutched the door knob. Her heart stopped. Simon Camden stood in the hall outside Katherine Stewart's dressing room. His hair glistened, and elegant evening clothes accentuated his tall, athletic build. He carried a top hat, and a black-satin cape hung over his arm.

He talked through the dressing room doorway. "All right, love, have a good show. I'll find you later, in the pub." He saw Elly and smiled. "Good evening, Miss Fielding." His voice was smooth as heavy cream.

She walked towards him. "Good evening, Mr. Camden." With soft fingers, he gently stroked her face. Her eyes closed and her stomach tightened.

"Is that Elly?" Katherine came to the door holding a costume coat. The girl guiltily jerked back and Simon chuckled. Unconcerned, Katherine shook her head. "Simon, you're incorrigible. Elly, is Connie in the costume shop?"

"She was a few minutes ago."

"Good. Be a dear and take this to her. The clasp still isn't right. It used to fall open, now it's so tight I can hardly get it undone."

"Yes, ma'am." Elly took the coat and hurried upstairs. The wardrobe mistress quickly adjusted the clasp, and Elly hurried out.

"Elly," Simon whispered from the shadows. Trembling, she went to him. He took the coat from her arms, pulled the rag from her hair, and ran his fingers through her thick copper mane. He slid an arm around her waist and seemed pleased to feel a supple young spine instead of the expected whalebone corset. He pulled her tight against him and kissed her, first lightly, then deeply. With the other hand, he stroked her cheek, then slid his fingers down her throat and over her breast. She felt a sweet pain as her body pressed against his. After a moment, he released her. "You'd better take that coat. M' Lady Katherine is waiting."

Without a word, she backed away. Still staring into his eyes, she turned to take the coat, stumbled over her own feet, and raced down the stairs.

Chapter 19

The next day was two performances of *The Magistrate*. Elly arrived at the theatre shortly before noon and chatted with Adams, the old stage-doorkeeper. They both stood to attention as Eric Bates came through the stage door, followed by Simon Camden.

Eric shook his head. "I believe everything you're saying, Simon, I'm just not hearing any guarantees. Hello Adams, Miss Fielding." He acknowledged each with a nod.

As the two men walked by, Simon squeezed Elly's hand. She bit her lip to keep from smiling. Climbing the stairs to Eric's office, Simon said, "There are never guarantees, Eric, but look at the past figures..."

Elly watched them go. "I'd better be off, Mr. Adams."

"All right, m' girl. Take care now."

She dragged herself up to wardrobe and spent a tedious hour sewing on buttons. When she accidentally stabbed herself and bled on the fabric, she was allowed to stop sewing and carry costumes downstairs. On the third floor, she walked out of a dressing-room, and lurched back.

Simon Camden appeared in front of her. "Easy there," he smiled. "I'm not going to hurt you."

She backed against the cold wall. Her eyes were wide, her breathing shallow and fast.

"But, I am going to touch you." He planted his hands on the wall, on either side of her shoulders, and slowly lowered his lips onto hers. His mustache and beard felt lovely, and his lips were soft as rose petals, caressing her, loving her. When he pulled away, she leaned forward, following him. He leaned into her again, this time with more pressure. She responded, her breasts heaving, rich with feelings, longing to be touched. The third time he kissed her, his lips opened, and his tongue gently caressed her lips. Hesitantly, her tongue joined his. One arm cradled her slender waist, pulling her tight against him. The other hand searched through heavy fabric, petting and squeezing her small, firm breasts, until the exquisite pain brought tears to her eyes.

Reaching behind her, he unhooked her frock and pulled it down around her waist. He kept her arms locked in the lowered sleeves, then pulled off her camisole and smiled at the sight of her young, supple breasts. She shivered with cold and fear, then groaned as his mouth, warm and moist, caressed her nipples. Quickly, they turned hard as acorns. She wanted to scream with pleasure. Releasing her arms, he let them pull out of her frock and stretch around his neck. He held her body tight against his.

When his hand reached under her skirt, tears of fright ran down her cheeks. "No. Please, No!" He held her tighter, kissing away her tears. He whispered reassuring nonsense into her ear, while gently pushing his fingers between her legs. She clutched his shoulders, gritting her teeth to keep from crying out. Keeping his mouth hard over hers, he rubbed through thin fabric, until her back arched, and her legs pulled hard together.

Smiling to himself, he lowered her to the floor and gently pulled off her drawers. She lay back trembling, as he raised her knees and spread her legs apart. His eyes never left her face as he unbuttoned his trousers. Sliding his fingers inside her, he smiled at her wetness.

"How sweet you are." He kissed her knees, the insides of her thighs and moved his tongue higher, until she lurched back, gritting her teeth to keep from screaming. Her heart was leaping out of her chest. She felt a searing pain the instant he entered her, then a sensation so exquisite she could only sob. He tightly embraced and kissed her as he entered her again-and-again. Through a clenched jaw, he groaned louder and louder, his face contorting as if in pain. Suddenly, he pulled out of her. Gasping for breath, and stifling a scream, his body cramped, then collapsed in an exhausted heap. They lay quiet for a few minutes.

When he had enough breath to speak, he said, "You deserve better than the hard wood floor. I hadn't planned it this way. I'm sorry. Are you all right?" She shivered with cold. He stood, pulled on his trousers, and helped her into her clothes. Her hair fell in a great copper fold, and he gently pushed it away from her face. "Elly," he lifted her chin and looked into her eyes. "Are you all right?" He was genuinely concerned. "Say something."

She tried to smile, but the words, "I'm fine," came out in a sob.

He held her tight and she clung to him, burying her face in his shoulder, inhaling his musky cologne. "You're not with child, I finished on the floor. At least you don't have to worry about that."

She whispered. "Thank you."

His mouth dropped open. "Oh, dear, she's polite at a time like this. My precious girl, I practically raped you, and you say, 'Thank you.'"

She laughed. "Oh, no Simon, that wasn't rape. I know what... That definitely wasn't..." Swallowing a sob, she took his face in her hands and kissed him. He held her lovingly.

Voices sounded below stairs and they guiltily pulled away from each other. She frantically smoothed her skirt. "I've got to fix my hair. Is the rest of me all right?"

He turned her around and nodded. She ran her fingers through his long, tousled hair, stroked his beard, hurried to her dressing room, and collapsed into a chair. Leaning her elbows on the dressing table, she put her head in her hands, waiting for her racing heart to slow. There were no stoves on the top floor. It was so cold she could see her breath. She looked into the mirror. Her hair was a mess, but a radiant blush flushed her cheeks, and she laughed. The soreness between her legs was slightly worrying, but she knew it would go away. Reliving Simon's touch, she closed her eyes. Even with the soreness, her body wanted more.

She ran a comb through her hair, quickly winding the copper mass up and out of the way. Grimy window glass rattled softly, and her feet made a sand dance as they slid under the table. The cracked walls were streaked with gray, and everything smelled of greasepaint and dust. She caught a reflection of her pale eyelashes and remembered Simon's thick blond lashes hovering over his gray eyes. Lady Richfield had said she should find a lover with experience, but Simon was Katherine Stewart's gentleman friend. *What have I done?* Her heart raced again. She swallowed a sob. *I can't tell anyone. Not ever.*

Robert's clear dark eyes shined in her memory. Remembering his sweet smile, his scent, and the feel of his soft lips, her body cramped again. *Could it be like that with Robert?*

She glanced back into the mirror, caught a reflection of an empty hanger, and remembered her employment. The costumes! She tore out of the door and down the stairs.

Chapter 20

Sunday, January 3, 1904

At first light, Sam Smelling kissed a green ribbon he had pulled from Elly's hair. "For luck." He folded it into his lapel pocket and shivered with dread. Tomorrow Robert Dennison was coming to London. If Anthony Roundtree had Robert followed, he would find Elly.

Valise in hand, four newspapers tucked under his arm, he boarded the 6:00 a.m. train at St. Pancras Station for Skipton, the southern tip of the Yorkshire Dales. As the nearly empty train left the station, Sam pulled out his notebook and reviewed rough maps Elly had drawn of her house and grounds. He silently repeated the unfamiliar name: *Elisa Roundtree, Elisa Roundtree, Elisa Roundtree.* He checked his list of targets:

1. Anthony Roundtree: *her father.*
2. Sir John Garingham: *her betrothed.*
3. Lillian Roundtree: *her maiden aunt.*
4. Dr. Frederick Vickers: *present at Elly's birth, her mother's death - signed the birth and death certificates.*
5. Elizabeth Graves: *witnessed her mother's marriage to Anthony Roundtree.*
6. Father Laurence Folen: *performed the marriage ceremony.*

The hypnotic train motion soothed him into a deep sleep. Before he knew what was happening, a grizzled trainman shook him awake. "Waike oop yoong man, your stop's next. Tha got t' change i' Bradford if yer wantin' Skipton. It's coomin' rait away!"

"Uh, thanks." The short ride to Skipton was on a smaller, less comfortable train.

The picturesque Skipton station was bright with afternoon light. Chilled to the bone, Sam hurried inside to a potbellied stove radiating warmth. The elderly stationmaster dozed with his feet on a chair. He leapt to attention and straightened his uniform. "Good day sir. How may I serve y'?"

Sam smiled cordially and warmed his hands. "I'm looking for Father Laurence Folen."

The stationmaster looked surprised. "Well sir, there's a Father Folen up Settle way." He leaned close, whispering, "Got in trouble and the bishop shipped him out to the moors. His wife left him an' all. Had no proper church for years now. Trots around on a pony, prayin' with folk in barns and sheep huts. No way o' knowin' where 'e might be. Y' might ask the Catholic priest Father Flynn, up at St. Ann's. He knows everybody."

Sam nodded. "I'm also looking for an elderly woman named Elizabeth Graves."

"Well the countryside is covered with folk named Graves, but I don't know a woman o' tha' name."

"I see. What about Dr. Frederick Vickers."

"That's an easy one. Runs a dispensary in the dales, near Grassington. Used to have a very good practice in town, very sociable fellow he was. Turned queer a few years back, prefers taking care of sheep farmers and the few miners still working. That's that last of Garingham's mines you know."

"How do I find Dr. Vickers?"

"Aye - well, t' train 'll take you on to Grassington. From there you'll need to 'ire a horse, or get a lift from a farmer."

Sam found Saint Ann's Church just as high mass was ending. Hungry and exhausted, he was very pleased when plump, elderly Father Tim Flynn invited him to dine at the rectory. Father Tim collapsed into an easy chair, yanked off his collar, and tossed it aside. "Aw, but those are hateful things. Sure I am the almighty didn't intend his priests t' live in a continual state of purgat'ry, but here we are. So, young man, what brings y' to Skipton?"

Sam sat on the sofa, opened his mouth to speak, and was covered with three huge, licking dogs. Wet noses, tongues, and violently wagging tails were everywhere.

"Hello, m' darlin's, here y' are, yes, yes!" Father Tim hugged and kissed a shorthaired black Labrador, a longhaired golden, and a third beast that seemed a cross between the two.

156

Enjoying the affection, but not the mess, Sam stood up. One by one, he held each dog by the collar, and pushed his rump, commanding him to, "SIT!"

Father Tim beamed. "Jasus, Mary, and Joseph, the good Lord's sent me a dog trainer."

During a delicious meal of roast beef and Yorkshire pud', Father Tim shared the local gossip. "Laurence Folen! Blessed Mother o' God, never thought anyone'd b' lookin' fer that scoundrel. A bit too fond of his choir boys he was. We all have our transgressions. Mind y', I'd rather transgress with the ladies," he winked an eye.

Sam smiled back. "It appears the Reverend Folen married a lady to a second husband before her first husband was dead."

"Yer joshin' me! Did Folen know the husband was living?"

"I'm not sure anyone knew."

"Can I ask the name o' the lady?"

"Bertha Roundtree."

"The Roundtrees from Settle?"

"The same."

"Anthony's wife?"

"...and Charles's."

Father Flynn lit his pipe. "I knew the Roundtree family, years ago. Albert Roundtree was a marvelous good lookin' man. His son Charlie was like him and the girl, Lillian. Young Anthony, Tony they called him, was a throwback o' some kind. Albert broke his neck fallin' from a horse. Charlie came into a lot o' money and took himself off to Hamburg to study engineering. Stayed there fer years gettin' in thick with a German firm, marrying the daughter. Tony was supposed t' be managin' the estate, but gambled it away, piece by piece. Charlie died workin' on the canal in Suez. Damn shame it was. After that, rumors came 'round about Tony keepin' fancy company. I heard tell about a daughter, but never a wife, so that was a mystery."

"It's no mystery anymore. The money belongs to Charles Roundtree's daughter. Anthony claims to be her father. Elisa's mother died in childbirth."

"...and now the girl wants her inheritance."

"Not a bit. She's hardly more than a child. Until a week ago, she thought she was penniless. She's betrothed to Sir John Garingham, hates him, and ran away from the marriage."

"Betrothed to Garingham? Blessed Mother o' God, isn't that perfect."

"Do you know Sir John Garingham?"

"Everyone knows Garingham. Years ago, the old Earl Edward Garingham owned everything and everybody. Miners hadn't been indentured for years, but woe betide the ones who tried to quit Garingham." He puffed slowly. "One by one, disaster struck the mines. Every few years one caved in, or give out. The son, John Garingham, was ruined with spoiling. The finest schools, expensive holidays in Scotland. I've heard he goes shooting with the king. The king mind y', and those boys do a good deal more than just shooting." He chuckled.

"I dare say you're right, but isn't that sort of expected, I mean, by men of that class?"

"Not if they got no money. It takes a lot of money to ramble with royalty."

"But the coal mines…"

Father Tim snorted. "Down to practically nothin', ten years ago at least. Just before Christmas the last good one collapsed up near Tebay."

Sam's heart was racing. "So there's no money coming in now?" Father Tim shook his head and Sam looked around the room. "Is there a telephone? I need to call London."

"Yes! I've just got one." Father Tim beamed. "Hardly ever been used. Never called London, this is marvellous."

"I'll pay you for the call."

"Nonsense, laddie. Teach me to make m' dogs sit. That'll be payment a plenty."

Sam gave the operator Isabelle's phone number. It took an hour for the call to go through. When Sam heard Isabella say that Elly was well, he breathed a sigh of relief.

The next morning, Sam bid Father Tim and his dogs goodbye, and caught a train to Grassington. The tiny station was deserted. He walked down a country lane for an hour before finding the village. The grocer was making a delivery to Dr. Vickers's dispensary, so Sam paid him for a lift. At 2:00 the grocer's boy loaded his cart. When it started to rain the boy headed for the pub. "Can't go now, road's too wet." At 4:30, the boy said, "Can't go now, be dark soon."

Sam spent the night in a room over the pub. Annoyed at having wasted an entire day, he bought a local paper and bored himself to sleep with the prices of wool and sheep dip.

Chapter 21

Monday, January 4, 1904

Grateful for a day off, Elly slept late, washed, dressed, and met Michael at the underground. She had never traveled on this small subterranean railroad. It was exciting. After a few stops, they were at South Kensington Station, Exhibition Road, practically in front of the Gildstein Gallery. A sign outside read:

Premier Exhibition:
ROBERT DENNISON
Oils and Pastels
January 5th - 10th

Elly held her breath as they walked up the three front steps and went inside. Just past a small reception area, they turned the corner. Elly nearly fainted. Directly in front of them, in an ornate gilded frame, hung *Autumn Lady*.

Michael caught his breath and grabbed her arm. The warm copper of Autumn Lady's hair flew wild against a background of mottled leaves. It was hard to tell if she was lying down or standing up, surrounded by brilliant clusters of reds and yellows. The intensity of her green eyes and the hint of a seductive smile held him captive. He pulled his eyes away from the painting long enough to look at the pale trembling girl on his arm.

"Rob looked at you and saw her? She's beautiful. No mistaking it's you, but..." he shook his head.

Elly silently prayed, *please God, don't let anyone else recognize me*. As they walked into the main room, she broke into a grin. Immaculately framed, hanging on pristine walls, were paintings she loved, and some she had never seen. She saw the school chapel with the river in the background. She could almost smell the fresh-cut grass and hear water running over the rocks. Hearing voices, she followed Michael toward a second room that housed the pastels. Workmen pulled a partition, shortening the space. Robert was concentrating on the construction and he did not see his friends. He wore his usual dark suit, but his shirt was new, and his tie was a bright combination of colors no school-master would ever wear.

A well dressed, elderly man directed the workers. "A little further chaps, that's it. Jake, mind your end."

"Sorry, Gov'." A man with matted yellow hair caught the partition just before it slammed into the wall.

Robert clutched Mr. Gildstein's hand in both of his. "This is a dream come true, sir. Thank you so much."

"You're a gifted painter, Mr. Dennison. I always said so. I'm only pleased no one else has been shrewd enough to give you a show before now. We'll make money together. Wait and see." He put a fatherly hand on Robert's shoulder, and saw Michael and Elly in the doorway. "Your friends?"

Robert turned. "Yes. Indeed they are." The three hurried toward each other, hugged and laughed. Robert introduced them to his benefactor.

Michael gave Robert a playful sock on the arm. "Rob, these paintings are marvelous. That picture of Elly is as good as anything in the National Portrait Gallery."

Mr. Gildstein nodded. "It's better than some." He waved goodbye, and walked past Jake, still fiddling with the partition.

Jake sunk onto his haunches, slowly turned his head, and settled his eyes on Elly. Silent as a snake, he slithered from the room.

Robert looked so handsome, and his smile was so inviting, Elly wanted to throw herself in his arms. Instead, she pretended to study his pictures.

Robert stared lovingly. "I've been looking at that painting, wondering if I'd dreamed you." She smiled shyly, but did not speak. He asked, "So... You're all right, then?"

She forced a big smile, but a black cloud seemed to cover her. *I am not all right. I'm trying to hide from my father, and a huge picture of me hangs in the foyer, for the entire world to see.* Robert waited. His soft brown eyes were full of concern. She clenched her jaw. *He risked everything for me. I have to risk this for him.* Squeezing her hands into fists at her sides, she took a deep breath. "Yes, thank you. I'm absolutely fine... And you?"

"Actually, I'm frightened to death."

Michael laughed. "Why? Mr. Gildstein just said that you'd make money together. He's the authority, isn't he?"

"Pray God, he's right." He looked back at Elly. "Oh, my sweet girl." He reached for her and she threw herself into his arms. They held each other tight. "You have no idea what that school was like without you. I have missed you so much." He kissed her forehead and cheeks. "The very thought of spending the rest of my life at a place like that..."

Michael threw up his hands. "Rob, it won't happen. This time next week, you'll have a slew of commissions and be setting up your own studio."

Chuckling softly, Robert let Elly go. "Thanks Mike. I needed to hear that. In fact, thanks for everything. You've been a rock."

"I haven't, actually. I became the world's worst coward when I got your second letter. Elly's made a lot of friends. You'll need to thank them."

Robert gave her a squeeze. "Have you really? That's wonderful. I want to hear everything that's happened."

After supper at a nearby pub, Michael took Robert and Elly to the room he rented in wig-master Eugene's large flat. They hung their coats by the front door, and Michael led them down a long hall leading to the bedrooms. He listened at one door and moved on, whispering. "That's my darling Sandra's room. She's playing Miranda in *The Tempest*. She's been on trains for two days and she's dead tired. I'll stay with her tonight. Here's my room. Sorry for the mess." He bid them good night, and left them alone.

Elly looked around the room. The wooden floor was bare and the white walls void of any decoration. A small desk was covered with books and scripts, and the bedcover lay crooked. She joked, "I'll wager Sandra's room looks better than this."

Robert's heart pounded. He opened his hands. "Elly, darling, you don't have to stay. I'll take you home this instant, if you want to go."

She looked at the floor. "I don't want to go, just yet."

He watched her for a moment, then walked over to the window, closed the drapes and hung on to them with both hands.

Elly's heart pounded. "Do you want me to stay?"

"More than anything. I wasn't sure you'd want to." There were tears in his voice.

"I, I want to talk." She gasped for breath. "Can we just… talk?"

"Oh, yes, please. That would be marvelous."

Chapter 22

Tuesday, January 5, 1904

It was two o'clock Tuesday afternoon when Sam Smelling finally arrived at the moorland dispensary of Doctor Frederick Vickers. The rustic medical center was clean, dry, and relatively warm. The walls were rough stone, and the roof was layered with thick slate. At first, Sam couldn't tell the doctor from his patients. Everyone wore heavy work boots and rough woven clothes. Only an intelligence behind his eyes, and long, clean, delicate fingers, made Dr. Vickers stand out from the rest. It was after 4:00 when the surgery emptied, and the doctor had a moment for Sam. "What can I do for you, sir?"

"You can tell me about the early morning of December 23, 1885."

A half-smile appeared on the doctor's face. "I've been waiting eighteen years for someone to ask me about that night. I'm famished. Let's have our tea."

After a tasty meal of pork pie and mushy peas, Dr. Vickers sat back with a tall glass of ale. "You saw the folks that came in today?"

Sam nodded, enjoying his glass of black stout.

"They are what they seem to be, nothing more and nothing less. Folks in the big houses, y' never know who you're dealing with." He laughed sadly. "It's taken eighteen years for someone to notice that something was wrong that night. Eighteen years. The worst night o' my life, the night that child was born. What's your interest?"

"The child, Elisa. She's eighteen and trying to escape marrying Sir John Garingham."

Dr. Vickers grimaced. "Good luck to her. That union was signed and sealed the moment she was born."

"You see nothing wrong in it?"

"I see everything wrong in it, but what's t' be done? That bastard, Tony Roundtree, married the mother, Bertha, before the child was born, so Elisa's his property. I'm surprised he didn't marry her off last year, at seventeen. Garingham paid off Tony's debts and promised to keep him on a generous allowance. In exchange, Garingham was to marry Elisa and get a share of her fortune."

"Did Bertha willingly marry Anthony Roundtree?"

"Oh, my grief, man. That poor woman was in such torment, she didn't know if it were day or night. She'd been in labor three days before they called me. Three days! They'd a good midwife, Betty Graves, she was the best there was."

"Where is she now?"

"Dead, long ago. But that baby was so twisted up inside, she wasn't skilled enough to handle that. After poor Bertha died, and I cut the child from her belly, I was sure she'd be deformed in some way. Year-after-year I was amazed to see her grow healthy and beautiful. I watched from a distance, mind y'. I wanted nothing more to do with that bastard Roundtree."

"Would you stand up in court and testify that Bertha Roundtree was not in a rational state of mind when she married Anthony Roundtree?"

He snorted a laugh. "Do you know how little my life would be worth, if I crossed Roundtree and Garingham together?" He paused, looking at the ceiling. "I wonder if anyone would believe me. What's the word of a country doctor against an earl and his father in-law?"

"They wouldn't go so far as murder, surely?"

"They may have already."

"What are you saying?"

"I had a patient, about ten years ago. Al Sanderson, been in the military, serving in Suez. His family was from Tebay, and they all worked in Garingham's mine. He came home, went back into the mines and a beam fell on him. On his deathbed, he told me that while he was in Suez, he got a letter from his sister saying that Garingham threatened to collapse a shaft on his whole family, unless he arranged for the murder of Charles Roundtree. The poor sod was a regular serviceman, no money or connections, his whole family in Tebay. Didn't know what else to do, so he gave a local thug a pound, and Charles Roundtree's body was found floating in the canal."

The blood drained from Sam's face. "May I make a call?" He walked to the telephone box in the corner.

"You may."

"I'll pay for the call."

"And being a poor country doctor, I'll accept payment. Please, help yourself."

Sam was already cranking the handle. He rang Isabelle, and the call went through in only a few minutes. Smythe answered, saying that Her Ladyship was out, not expected home until late, and His Lordship was in Kent. Her Ladyship had specifically wanted Mr. Smelling to know that all was well with Elly Fielding. After leaving Dr. Vickers's number, Sam asked Smythe to tell Isabelle that Elly Fielding was in danger and needed protection immediately. Smythe promised to leave the message where Her Ladyship would see it, directly upon her return. Sam thanked him and hung up.

Shaken, he turned back to Dr. Vickers. "This man, Sanderson... is his sister still around?"

"Couldn't say. Never knew her."

"Roundtree's sister, Elisa's Aunt Lillian. What's she like?"

"A frightened rabbit. Worst fate in the world, the spinster sister of a mean-spirited brother. Nowhere to go, totally dependent. I've heard he beats her."

Sam looked grim. "Tell me about Reverend Laurence Folen."

"That old sodomite! What do you want to know?"

"I want to know about that night." Sam sat down, ashen.

Dr. Vickers smirked. "Roundtree had found Folen with his stable boy and threatened to tell the Bishop. Folen did what he was told."

"Even going so far as to commit bigamy?"

"What?"

"In all probability, Charles Roundtree was still alive on December 23."

Dr. Vickers started laughing and did not stop until tears ran down his cheeks.

*

After Smythe hung up the telephone, he wrote a very careful note:

Your Ladyship,
Sam Smelling called from Grassington 9 - 8, at 6:00 this evening. He wants you to know that Elly Fielding is in danger and needs protection immediately.
Smythe

He took the note upstairs to Isabelle's boudoir, pulled a chair in front of the door, and placed the note on the chair, so she could not possibly miss it. An hour later, Cindy and Bella raced down from the nursery with armloads of pictures they had painted for their mummy. Knowing that her mistress was out for the evening, the accompanying nanny opened the door to the boudoir. The little girls ran past her and plopped their paintings on a chair that had conveniently been left in front of the door.

Chapter 23

Wednesday, January 6, 1904

The alarm clock rang and Robert groaned. "What's the time?"

"Seven." Elly kissed him good morning and reset the clock for eight-thirty.

He pulled the cover over his head, disappearing into the warm darkness.

Elly climbed off the bed, still in her rumpled frock. The coal fire had gone out hours ago and the floor was like ice. Shivering, she pulled on her shoes and coat, wrapped her scarf around her hair, tiptoed from the flat, downstairs, and outside to the quiet residential street. The omnibus stop was a five-minute walk. It was still dark, and very few people were about. Today was the first rehearsal of *The Tempest*. She planned to have breakfast at the boardinghouse, change into a fresh frock, and get to rehearsal before ten.

"Autumn Lady." It was a man's voice.

She froze, then quickened her pace.

A man stepped in front of her. "Didn't you hear me call you, Autumn Lady?"

She recognized Jake, the gallery worker with the matted yellow hair. Relieved to see a familiar face, she released her breath. "Oh, good morning. You startled me." He stood squarely in front of her, his arms behind his back. A harsh gust of wind pushed her off balance, and blew his yellow hair oddly askew. Forcing a smile, she looked into his steely eyes. Her voice sounded hoarse. "That's a lovely painting, but I assure you, I wasn't the model."

The wind blew again, pushing his hair further over his face. He made no attempt to straighten it. He was wearing a wig. His lips spread into a sneer, revealing the gap from a missing tooth. "Yorkshire lassies shouldn't tell lies."

Elly's eyes grew huge. She lunged sideways and ran back toward Michael's flat. Jake followed, cursing under his breath. She passed a narrow alley without seeing a huge man standing in the shadows.

Jake yelled, "Catch her, Mick!"

The huge man grabbed her from behind. She flayed her arms and legs, screaming at the top of her lungs. Jake forced a foul smelling cloth over her face. Her kicking legs gave way, as she lost consciousness.

End of Book Two

Made in United States
North Haven, CT
03 January 2023

30575048R00102